The Case
of the
Great Train
Robbery

The Case of the Great Train Robbery

A Sean Sean Mystery

Brookins Books

The Case of the Great Train Robbery

A Brookins Books Paperback

ISBN 978-0-9853906-0-0
Cover: John Toren
Cover photo: Carl Brookins

The characters and events in this novel are fictional and created out of the imagination of the author. Real locations and institutions are mentioned, but the characters and events are entirely fictional.

Printed in the United States of America

1

He raised the short piece of pipe over his head and rushed me. When he got within range he swung it. The guy aimed it at my head. A mistake. He could have broken my arm. Instead he missed because I ducked and kicked him in the crotch as hard as I could. It was one of the few times when I wished I was wearing hard-soled shoes instead of my usual red Keds. The ones with the soft white soles. Still, he went down in a heap, screaming in agony and clutching his groin. Tears came and I could see the flash of silver in his back molars. I hoped his yells didn't disturb the neighbors. He'd showed up while I was scoping out the back yard of a former lake cottage right across the road from White Bear Lake. On the north side of that pond.

This area has a history, if you're interested in crime in the nation. Back in the old days, in a previous century, before urban development filled in all the open spaces, if you were an active bank robber working in Ohio or Illinois, let's say, and the G-men or the local constabulary was getting a little too close to nabbing you, you looked for a hideout. You wanted someplace where you weren't easily recognized to lay low and let the heat die down. So you and your gang might decide on a few weeks of R & R in a quiet, anonymous lake place, nestled among the tall fragrant pines of Minnesota or Wisconsin. The stories are that a number of gangsters did just that. Nice folks like Ma Barker, Al Karpis and good ol' John Dillinger, not to forget that dashing man about town, Al Capone.

This particular back yard where I was now standing over a moaning thrashing thug was attached to a nice-looking house that had started out as one of those lake cottages. Back in the nineteen 'twenties. Back in that time, as long as you didn't cause too much trouble by knocking over speakeasies or gunning down troublesome rivals on the streets of St. Paul, the local cops would leave you pretty much alone while you rested. It was a tidy arrangement. At least it was for the cops and robbers. Ordinary citizens didn't think much of the deal. They didn't really care to be rubbing shoulders with the odd murderer or bank robber when they went shopping at Scheunemann's Department Store or picking up a midday snack at George's Popcorn and Candy down at the corner of Wabasha and Seventh Street.

Anyway, back then, after a little rest, you'd clean your arsenal, acquire some fresh ammunition, 'cause you wanted to avoid miss-fires in tense times. Then you'd climb into your Ford flivver or your posh Packard and toddle off back to the grimy streets of Chicago, or Des Moines, or maybe Omaha, or some little town in between where you heard they had a bank ripe for the plucking. Or maybe you'd check out a train that could be heisted out on the plains with not too much law around to interfere.

That semi-official protection system, instituted by some of the same good folks who brought you the Irish potato famine, didn't last too long, partly because a few shortsighted thugs, who maybe got to feeling they hadn't amassed their fair share of ill-gotten loot from previous escapades, decided to pull a job or two right here in St Paul. Easy pickins', they might have figured. Or, maybe they just got bored with the peaceful life. I mean, if you're a hot-shot gangster in flashy spats and a cool pin-stripe double-breaster, with a couple of Colt .38s weighing down your greasy armpits, sitting on a dock watching the waves roll in might get a little tedious. Boring, playing poker or Black Jack all day. So you got your buddy and pulled a couple of jobs. Then the whole stack of cards fell over faster than John Dillinger and his floozie boogied out of that St. Peter Street walkup the day the G-Men showed up, Tommy guns blazing.

Of course, times have changed and now that slightly seedy-looking ex-lake cottage, former summer residence of the likes of Ma Barker or Baby Face Nelson, had been rehabbed, repainted, expanded and fixed up, probably a couple of times. It had become a fairly substantial middle-class home. Like this one. For all I knew, some of those very same notorious criminals of yore might have stayed in this place back then.

It wasn't history that brought me to this back yard this fine summer day. The present owner, not the guy lying on his back moaning on the wet grass and clutching his crotch, had decided to do a little fixing up of his own. What Mr. Kent Kava, present owner, had wanted to do was to repair, or maybe replace, the dilapidated old garage at the back of the property. It was a project right up his alley, as it were, Kava being something of a handyman. The garage wasn't in use at the time, except for storage. Hadn't been a real garage for quite some years, apparently. So there wasn't any hurry. Kava was a guy not only handy with tools but he was a trained professional architect. He could design a whole new garage, if he wanted to go that far. But what he really wanted was just to clean out the accumulated junk, tear down, haul away, shore-up, paint, repair, et cetera, et cetera. Or so he'd laid it out for me one day in my office.

He and his family, he said, had already lived in the place for over a year when he got this wild hair about his garage. Or maybe his wife got on him about it. I didn't know and really didn't care all that much. I didn't think it was relevant. No, he said, in answer to my question. He hadn't had any problems with the neighbors when he started carting stuff out. A few strangers occasionally came to the door, of course, like that vacuum-cleaner salesmen, and a wandering evangelist or two. The usual. Kava was a freelance architect and small-time builder, he repeated, and he worked at home, except when he was on a construction site or seeing a client somewhere. His wife had a job in a downtown bank in St. Paul and son Alex went to school. Nice middle class family. No problems; an even-tenored life the Kava family led. Not even any serious disagreements at home, to hear him tell it.

Until he started on the garage. At first, when it was just cleaning up and carting junk away, things went fine. Took him two months, he said, to clean it out. But then he decided some of the rafters were seriously deteriorating, apparently from a leaky roof. So he started tearing off the shingles. Demolishing. Exposing old beams. Then people passing by could see what he was doing and his project became more widely known. Idle chatter commenced. Traffic of strangers increased. How much demolishing was he going to do? Would he tear the entire structure down? Did he know it was a really old garage and this part of the city was sort of an historic neighborhood? Was he going to pour a concrete foundation? Seemed a few folks with too much time on their hands were meeting in the local coffee shops and small stores and one of their subjects for idle speculation was Kava's garage project.

"I was advised that in White Bear I needed a permit to tear down and replace my old garage," he explained in one of our talks. "So of course, that made my project even more public."

I nodded. "Sure. Building permits are part of the public record."

Eventually, Kava went on, a couple of gentlemen showed up who wanted to inspect the property. Closely inspect the property. They even intimated they'd like to take a gander inside the house, as well as the garage, since they were in the neighborhood anyway. As it were.

Mr. Kava politely declined to allow them into the home, once he learned they had no particular legal basis for an inspection. In fact, he told me, he declined to allow them into the garage. "I didn't mind that they stood in the driveway and looked in. By then the garage was empty. But I didn't think it was a good idea to have them pushing on the walls, or kicking the studs. Didn't seem to be their business, after all."

"I understand," I said. "Did these stud-kickers have identification from the city?"

"They didn't show me anything."

"Any identification at all?"

"Sorry," Kava admitted. "I guess I never asked."

Just a couple of interested amateur historians, they said, and promptly backed off when questioned closely. Right. It was odd and strange and Kava began to wonder what was so special about his old garage, especially after he had had to chase someone off the place at about two a.m. one night. Being of a naturally skeptical bent, I would have been considerably more than just idly curious about all this curiosity. But I don't want to get ahead of myself here. That prowler incident had happened a week before he and son Alex showed up in my office. What brought him to my office was a discovery made beside the garage by the boy's puppy.

A brief introduction is called for. My name is Sean Sean. That's right. I have the same first and last name. So when strangers approach, on a train, perhaps, they aren't sure how familiar they're being. If my first name was Carl, say, it would be odd to approach me, a stranger, as Mr. Carl. So people sometimes hesitate. That occasionally gives me a slight advantage. I don't have a middle name. Sean NMI Sean, private investigator, at your service. On the other hand, there is a mystery writer whose last name is Carl. Lillian Carl. Anyway, as a private operative I have an office in Minneapolis. I'm not the most expensive, nor the least. I do work for some very important people in the Twin Cities, as well as for people nobody ever heard of.

Folks in the Twin Cities have the same kinds of problems and difficulties as people anywhere. We really aren't very different, here in the middle of the country. Maybe we have more blue-eyed blonds. We are frequently just as sophisticated and nice, and just as underhanded and mysterious as anybody. You'll see what I mean.

2

So, what got me to the back yard of the Kava place in White Bear Lake and my confrontation with this thug now rolling on the grass in pain, all started a week or so earlier. I was in my place of business. The young gentleman who walked into my office with a revolver didn't appear dangerous at first glance. Indeed since he was smaller than I am, I stayed pretty calm.

"Are you Mr. ... Sean?" He inquired. There's that problem with my name.

The guy looked at me with those big blue eyes from under a very blond, very unruly mop of hair. He was slender and he was carrying a cardboard box. He was young. Behind him stood another short man, also slender, with sandy hair, a sharp nose and heavy black-framed glasses. He was stoop shouldered and reminded me vaguely of the film guy, Woody Allen.

"Yes, sir," I said to the boy with the box, "I am he. Sean Sean." Since the boy, who I judged was about twelve, was the one who had asked, I continued to look at him. I smiled. My disarming smile. The one I practice. I waited. I often do that. A lot of people are uncomfortable with silence so they fill it with talk. Frequently what they say to fill the quiet spaces is more revealing than their prepared speeches, or their answers to the questions posed.

"My name is Kent. Kent Kava." From the taller, Woody Allen type. "This is my son Alex." The family resemblance was fairly obvious.

I stood and shook the proffered hand. Kent Kava? Was his wife's name Kate, I wondered to myself? I hoped not. My lady love is named Catherine and I didn't want to take a case with names that could confuse me. I didn't ask, though. I just waited some more. Kent looked at me, apparently waiting for his son to proceed. Finally I waved at the two chairs and sat down in my own desk chair. My office isn't all that large, but I don't need much space and we three were now occupying most of it. Alex slid into his chair and immediately pulled his legs up. Youngsters can do that fairly easily. He glanced intently around the office. I couldn't tell what he was thinking. I transferred my gaze to his father. When I said he was short, I meant shorter than most of the population of North America. But he was taller than me. I'm shorter than most adult people in the entire world. I was taller than his son.

I was getting tired of waiting for Kava to get on with it. Time is money, and all that. "Is there something a private detective can do for you gentlemen today?"

Kava senior nodded and took the box from his son and dropped it on the desk between us. It made a satisfying thunk when it landed. It was an ordinary dark brown box, probably a shoebox. He looked at his son and said, "Tell Mr. Sean what you found, Alex."

Alex looked at his dad, looked at me and licked his lips. Then he told me the story he had obviously rehearsed a couple of times. "I have a puppy. Spot? We live in White Bear and my daddy is tearing down this old garage in our yard. Spot likes to dig in the ground, especially around the garage where it's loose and there isn't much grass. Mama yells at Spot when he digs in the lawn. I let him dig all the time, but my mom says he tracks dirt in the house, so I'm supposed to watch him and clean his feet first. Before we go back in the house or anything."

"I see," I said.

"Anyway, day before yesterday Spot was digging in the dirt and he found this." Alex pointed at the box and glanced at his dad.

"I took it to my mom and she made me put it down. My dad was at the store." He stopped; obviously satisfied he'd done his part.

Kent Kava nodded and tapped his son on the arm. "When I came home a few minutes later, this was lying on the back porch." With a small sense of the dramatic, Kava whisked the top off the box and we all peered inside. Lying there was a revolver, or what was left of one. An old .38 caliber revolver with about an eight-inch barrel, I judged. I have some familiarity with handguns and my educated guess would prove to be dead on.

The weapon was very dirty and exceedingly rusty on the frame and on the barrel. Most of the hand grips were missing. From my position, with the barrel pointing my way, I could also see that it was loaded. It was an old weapon. In its current condition it was dangerous, even if the trigger and hammer were frozen with rust. Or not. I'd have to ask some weapons expert about that. In case I ever encountered another rusty old handgun. I gently pushed the box around so the barrel of this weapon was pointed in a different direction, away from all of us, and said, "You should call the cops and they'll take it off your hands."

Kava nodded. "I suppose they would. If I tell them about it."

My ears perked up at that and then when he went on to explain about the people who had started coming by and showing interest in his garage project, my curiosity was definitely elevated. That too is one of my shortcomings, according to Catherine, my previously-referred-to lady friend. I am often too curious about too many things which shouldn't concern me.

Questions arose. Day before yesterday, Kent Kava had said his son found the piece. Now it's in my office. Why didn't they immediately call the White Bear Police? What was twelve-year-old Alex Kava doing in my office with the revolver? Sure, he found the thing and he was with his father, but still, it was a bit odd. There wasn't anything else in the box, there was hardly any dirt. I didn't ask these questions then. I find that sometimes the illogical has a perfectly ordinary explanation. But sometimes there's something else there. I've lost clients by asking the wrong question too early in the game. But my antennae were definitely vibrating.

The long and short of it was that Mr. Kent Kava wanted to hire me to find out what there was to be learned about the revolver, whatever else might be buried with it, and why there seemed to be more than a passing interest in the Kava garage project.

"I take it you didn't dig any further down or around in the hole where the puppy unearthed this weapon?"

"That's right. I threw a tarp over the hole and set a plank on top."

Monumental lack of curiosity, I thought. Or maybe not. We settled on the details, he gave me a check for a retainer, which my banker would be pleased to see, and they left my office, leaving behind the rusty revolver. I shook hands with both Kava and his son when they departed.

After they left, I took the cover off the box again and stared at the revolver for a little while. It didn't move at all. Nor did it suggest any startling insights. I hadn't expected it to. I knew that soon I would take the weapon to an expert to find out more. Weapons, my BCA friend Ann Hoover had told me, could be very informative. Age, caliber, dust and dirt clinging to the crevices, the manufacturer and associated ammunition all could provide a plethora of leads for the inquisitive examiner.

But for now I would lock it away in my snazzy new office safe, a gift from my main squeeze, Catherine, after an inquisitive cretin wrecked an earlier one. I was uncertain about how stable the ammo might be. Or how unstable. There were four bullets in the revolver's chamber and one spent cartridge. I tilted the container so light from my desk lamp filled the box. Closer inspection assured me I was right. It was a .38 caliber revolver. It looked like an old Navy Colt from right around the turn of the century. The previous century.

* * * *

Oh yeah, the guy in the yard? The one I had to disable with a hard shot to his crotch? I don't own a cell phone so I was going to have to secure this fellow before I went to the house to have Kava call the police. I grabbed the moaning felon by the shoulder and dragged him closer to my car. Then I fished a couple of large cable ties out of the trunk. You can buy plastic cable ties in most any hardware store and they're cheaper than a set of handcuffs. And you don't have to keep track of a key. They make excellent temporary restraints. I yanked the guy's arms together and slipped a pair of the ties around his wrists. I knew he could eventually work his way out of them, given enough unsupervised time, but I wasn't about to give him that kind of opportunity. I wanted him off my hands and in custody as soon as possible. After I secured his wrists, I put another cable tie around his ankles. Then I pushed him over on his side so I could finish frisking him. In a back pocket he had a wallet with a few bucks in it but no ID. Nothing to identify him. Interesting.

I shoved the wallet back in his pocket and let my fingers do their thing, prodding him here and there where there might be something concealed, including his bruised crotch. By now he'd recovered somewhat from his painful encounter with my foot and cold and surly appeared to be the temperature of the day.

I stood back and looked at him. "Well, buddy, I think I'm gonna have the local cops come and haul you away. Unless of course you want to tell me who you are and why you jumped me. I admit what you tell me probably won't change my mind about calling the cops, though." I glanced around and located the short length of pipe my assailant had been brandishing. I considered poking the guy with it. There was a bang as the screen door on the back of the house closed. Evidently Kava heard the guy scream and had finally come out to see what was happening. Spot came along too. With a snuffle and a snort Kava's puppy ran up to us. Instantly he was all over the thug, licking, wagging, welcoming. Shows you that doggy instinct isn't always to be trusted. Me, the dog ignored.

"Kent?" I called.

"Sean? What's going on?"

"I have an intruder here. Would you call the cops to come get him?"

My client hesitated, then turned and without a word went back inside. I hoped the cops didn't come with sirens and lights. We didn't need any mid-day uproar. I stared at my captive. He was wearing black low-rise boots with hard heels and narrow square toes. I reached down for his ankle and he flinched back. I was quicker and hauled on his boot. It slid off in my hand and I discovered a plastic card inside. Gosh! It was his Minnesota Drivers License. Harlan Ford was qualified as a Class D driver, having paid the fee and passed requisite tests, and he even had a motorcycle endorsement. He turned out not to be an organ donor and he was a stated 32 years of age. His picture on the front made him look like a thug.

I slid the license into his shirt pocket and patted his cheek which earned me a snarl. A patrol car showed up and the officer took Mr. Ford into custody. First the officer verified my identity and bona fides with his boss back at HQ. I gave him a report and he hauled Mr. Ford off to the pokey. By now the afternoon sun was closer to the western horizon than to the eastern and I was faced with the prospect of a night in the Kavas' back yard.

3

Back to the beginning of this strange caper. After Kava pere et fils left my office and I locked away in my safe the weapon his son's puppy had found, I called a man I know at the Minneapolis police department. He's a homicide investigator with a long and impeccable reputation. Sergeant Ricardo Simon is also a good friend. Plus, he knows just about everybody in most of the police agencies around Minneapolis, or he knows somebody who knows somebody.

I know a lot of people myself, but it happens I had no contacts in the White Bear PD and it was looking like developing such an acquaintance might be a good idea. I try not to project that macho posture you see in some private investigators who don't want to cooperate with the local cops. Why they feel that way, I'm never quite sure. There are things the cops can do better and often faster than I. If I have a reasonable connection, that is. So I try to maintain such reasonable relationships. Simon got back to me in an hour with a reference and I called the man. Turned out he was the second highest honcho on the force in White Bear. Conveniently, he was at his desk. Also conveniently, he'd already had a conversation with my bud, the aforementioned investigator first class Ricardo Simon.

I explained in elliptical and non-specific language that I had a client living in his town and I gave him a few facts, very few. When the captain demurred, I justified my reticence under client privilege. We both knew there is no such thing when it applies to private investigators and their clients, but it's sometimes a handy device for both sides. He knew Ricardo and trusted him so I could proceed after he gave me the usual speech about rights, weapons, trespass and so on.

So that's why, a day after that meeting in my office in Minneapolis, I was in a position to be attacked by a thug in a yard just across a road from the shore of White Bear Lake. Specifically in Kent Kava's back yard. I was provoked. The feeling of provocation lasted after the cops transported felon Ford. Now I felt I needed some more answers. I'm not happy flailing around in the dark. There are enough mysteries in life. I prefer my cases to be clean and neat. Look at the crime scene, figure out the motive, go track the mope who did the dirty deed and either call in the cops or bag the guy myself. Here, I had many questions. So I went up on the back porch and rapped on the screen door with my heavy coprap. The one that sounds like I have all the authority in the world. I don't practice it very much because it can make my hand sore if I get too enthusiastic.

Kava came to the door. This time the puppy wasn't with him.

"We need to talk," I said

He hesitated and then sort of sagged his shoulders. He didn't have the greatest posture to start with. I suspected he'd been anticipating my questions for a while. "Yes, I suppose you are right," he mumbled. "Let me get something to drink and we'll sit out at the picnic table."

Sounded like a move to get his act together but what the Hell.

"Can I get you something?"

"Sure," I responded. "Thwarting guys trying to bash me on the head is thirsty work. I'd take a glass of water. Thanks."

He disappeared and a minute later came back out and handed me a plastic container of designer water. He was holding a sweating beer bottle. As the day went on, the humidity was rising, along with the temperature. We walked to the table. I chose to sit with the sun at my back. After Kava settled on the bench opposite me I cracked the twist top on my water and we each had a swig from our separate bottles. I said, "It's time to give me a little more background here. I don't think I can help you very much unless you tell me what's going on."

"But I don't know any more than you do." He squinted at me, put his hand up to shade his eyes.

"Okay, let's see if I've got this right. Puppy digs up a revolver and when you go to cover the hole you see other stuff in the ground. Right?"

Kava shrugged. Now, some people maintain that shrugs are non-committal. But I think the context matters. I think a shrug can be sarcastic, or impatient or even sympathetic. This one was sort of non-committal. Like he was telling me maybe he saw something and maybe he didn't, but without words. No commitment one way or the other.

"You found the gun and your son pointed out the location of the dig, right? That was at least a couple of days ago. And here we are but you don't seem to have the least bit of curiosity about what else may be in the hole. Or where the weapon may have come from."

Kava nodded.

"Upon finding a revolver, most people would call the cops. You didn't."

Nod.

"What's more, your wife didn't call the cops either."

"I got back from the store before she even had time to consider it."

Ah, he could still talk. "And what was that business in my office with Alex? You let a child carry a dangerous weapon around. Is that normal behavior for you?"

"Dangerous? How? I just let him carry it in and put it on your desk. He found it, after all."

"What if he'd dropped it or something else had set it off? Are you claiming that you don't know that old ammunition can be unstable? Or that the thing was loaded?"

He blanched and frowned. "No, I didn't know that. I assumed it was useless, that the gun wouldn't fire. I certainly didn't know it was loaded. I didn't examine the thing. I don't like guns and neither does my wife."

It seemed to me his concern for his son's welfare was genuine. "All right. Why didn't you or your wife call the cops to come get the gun?"

Kava shook his head and took a long swig of beer. Stalling.

I waited. I'm good at that. I can out-wait the best of them.

Finally he sighed and said, "Okay, I guess there's no way around this. First off, we've already had more curiosity than we want from neighbors, and a lot of other people we don't even know, about this stupid garage project. Kristi and I, we're very private in our life. That's the main reason I work by myself. I could make more money if I was hooked up with a big architectural or construction firm in the city but we like our independent quiet life. We want to keep our privacy.

"Kristi is the same way. Her job in the bank doesn't bring her into contact with the public and she likes it that way. We have very few friends and we just don't socialize much at all."

I could attest to that. I did a little checking on my client. I always do that. Helps keep me from being blindsided by things I could have anticipated had I only known...whatever. So I checked and discovered that the Kavas were indeed only a step or two above recluse. They might have been more comfortable in a cave in the mountains a million miles from anybody else. Their choice. Kava hailed from a mining family on the range, that large area of northern Minnesota where most of the iron ore they used to make steel in World War II came from. I hadn't yet explored his wife's family in any depth. Her first name started with a K, I noted.

"So we talked it over and decided that we'd hire an investigator to try to discreetly take care of the revolver and maybe bury everything else."

Interesting choice of words. "I guess I can buy that. Why bring your son to my office?"

"He found the damn thing, and he was kind of excited about it. We just figured that if he came along and told how he found it, and heard you explain a little of what you were going to do to track down the reason the gun was in my back yard, he'd be less likely to talk about it all over the neighborhood or at school."

I nodded my understanding. Then I wondered if little Alex had many friends. Not my problem. I wasn't as hopeful as Kava was that his strategy would work, but that was not something I had to be concerned about, so long as I didn't add to his worry. "Okay. Now I'm going to uncover the place the puppy dug and see what else is there. I'll just dig a deeper hole and try not to make a mess."

Kava rose. "Good. I guess you'll let me know what you find. I hope you can manage it before Kristi returns home from work." With that he went off back into the house. He was, I decided, a strange dude. His lack of curiosity was either forced or he was born with a missing gene. Or maybe he'd had a bad experience. I went to my car and hauled out a small spade I keep in the trunk for just such occasions along with one of those ubiquitous blue plastic sheets. I also picked up my digital camera. Come to think on it, I couldn't remember the last time I had to dig up some real dirt, but there you are. I still remember how.

I spread the tarp on the grass beside the boards Kava had placed there and then looked all around. The late afternoon critters were twittering and rustling in the bushes at the back of the property a few feet away and I realized I hadn't had any lunch. There hadn't been any city codes about building setbacks when the garage was first put up, so the big old lilacs that edged the property were close. Some of the branches pushed against the back of the building. The garage wall kind of leaned like it was pushing back against the lilacs. The site of the hole was about two-thirds of the way down the length of one long side of the structure. The side that faced into the yard. The hole was on the outside of the wall. For privacy, I sort of wished it had been in the garage. Which had only a dirt floor. On the other hand, a closer look at the partially deconstructed garage suggested I'd be safer outside in the fresh air.

Kava had said that the grass had always grown right up to the board siding of the garage and he regularly mowed it during the first summer they owned the place. He couldn't recall if there had been anything different about the area the dog had sniffed out. I wondered why the dog had chosen that particular spot in which to dig, and why that particular day, but those were questions I figured I would never get answers to. The puppy was like its masters—close mouthed.

I dragged the two wide boards off the hole. It wasn't more than a shallow indentation. The ground was loose and gave off a pleasant earthy smell. It was damp. It looked like someone, prob-ably Kava, had shoved the loose earth from the puppy dig back into the hole. I looked at the dark brown dirt for a moment. Then I eased the blade of my small spade into the hole at one edge. Almost immediately it struck firmer ground below the puppy's scratch depth. I shoved the blade in an inch and pried a chunk of hard dirt out of the hole. I proceeded around the perimeter of the hole, except where the side of the garage interfered. I sifted the dirt I had dug up through my fingers. Aside from a few small rocks it was just ordinary-looking soil.

I went around the perimeter again, standing on the shovel to drive it deeper, until I had a little trench. Then I shoved the spade hard at an angle into the hole from my little trench so the blade went down and toward the center of the dig. My thrust felt dif-ferent. The ground wasn't quite as hard. I gently pried. The spade had definitely struck something that didn't feel like soil. But it wasn't rigid either. So I pried some more. This time the spade loosened more than dirt and other stuff popped up on the shovel blade. Raggedy pieces of paper. I snatched one and brushed the damp clay off it. The edges crumbled easily but what I had looked like some mighty fine engraving like you might find on the corner or edge of an important document of some sort. Then I knew what it was. Money. Paper money. I was holding the moldering edge of what had once been a bank note. I set the spade aside and began to dig in the hole with my hands. Soon I was brushing the muck carefully aside and scooping out handfuls of loosened dirt. More engraved scraps of paper came to view. There was a lot of it. All of it was in pretty bad shape, but some of the colors were still apparent. Red and green. Greenbacks, maybe? Then I came across a piece of canvas. Looked like part of a bag. I'd discovered a bag of cash. Buried treasure. Money. Legal tender. But was it? And there had been an old revolver buried with it. Hot damn! This was some serious stuff here. I wondered if there was a reward for whatever loot I had unearthed. It just might be worth a night of being the duty watchman.

4

"I have an appointment in the city," Kent said, the next morning. "Kristi and I are riding in together. We're going to drop Alex and Spot at Alex's aunt's in Little Canada. I see you've covered the hole with the tarp. Turn up anything of interest yesterday?"

I hesitated. I didn't think Kava noticed. "Not really," I said, "but I'll do some more digging this morning."

He nodded, apparently satisfied, and went off. I yawned and stretched, watched the three of them loading young Alex's bike into the back of their station wagon. If Kava had noticed I spent the night in my car in his back yard, he didn't mention it. I had just decided, one of those split-second decisions, that I wasn't going to tell him about the rotted fragments of paper money I'd found yesterday. There were too many holes in the fabric the Kavas had woven for me.

When they left, Alex waved at me. The adults didn't. They disappeared in a westerly direction around the lake.

A while later, after I'd gone down to the nearby McDonald's for an egg sandwich, I took my ease on the bench beside the picnic table and thought about this case and my possible courses of action. One of my early moves had to be a conversation with Mrs. Kristi Kava, my client's wife, but I would need to do some spade-work first.

I picked up my spade and went back to the tarp-covered excavation for a different kind of digging. An hour later I felt pretty sure I had recovered everything in the hole that might be of any relevance. I looked at my watch and then at the detritus on my tarp. After my initial find, I'd dumped the dirt off the tarp and instead used the plastic to hold the fragments I was unearthing. The dirt went onto a pile on the grass beside the garage. It did occur to me that I might be disturbing long-buried evidence. Police forensics probably should have been called in, or maybe the historical society, but I figured that the puppy's initial dig and the boy's recovery of the pistol had pretty well destroyed any significant evidence, other than what we'd already found.

Muscles in my back and shoulder were sending messages telling me to quit with the physical labor. So I did.

What I had, and what I was able to reconstruct, sort of, from the fragments before me was that a long time ago somebody or several somebodies had buried a canvas bag of cash, amount undetermined, along with the revolver, in a hole in the ground beside the garage. There might have been other paper as well. Some of the tiny chewed up and rotted scraps could have been bonds, or other legal tender. I thought most of it was currency of some kind. The long burial had seriously damaged the paper I collected and I couldn't identify it. Maybe it was Canadian. Some of the fragments had the tell-tale green tinge of American bills. The largest fragment I located was maybe an inch by a quarter. Think irregular confetti. Some of this stuff was red and purple. What I did calculate was that this was definitely the remains of a crime. What kind of crime was a little uncertain. The stuff was booty because the quality of the engraving that I could see was first class. People just don't bury high-quality engraved paper that was most likely paper currency with a weapon unless laws have been broken. But even after I sifted through the pile of fragments, I only had partial letters, a number here or there, and scraps of what might have been canvas. And it stunk. It all smelled really bad.

From the evidence I deduced that a canvas bag with leather

corners had originally contained the paper, because I found part of a leather corner. The rivets were gone. There weren't any coins at all. I didn't want to clean any of it without some expert help because it was disintegrating almost before my eyes. So I packed it all carefully into a plastic trash bag I had in the car and stowed it in my trunk.

I was making certain assumptions. I assumed the smelly paper had once been money and it and the revolver were from some crime, like maybe a bank heist sometime in the past. I made those assumptions because that's the way I work. Besides, if this was all a big innocence, why was I here in the first place?

How far back this assumptive crime lay, I had no clue at the moment. And with no specific evidence of a crime, I could be off base. I mean, hey, maybe some eccentric guy just buried his money and his revolver one day to hide it from his wife. What did I know?

I left a note on Kava's back door and departed. First I went home and cleaned up, had a little lunch and called my honey. Catherine Mckerney owns and operates a thriving massage school in Minneapolis. In addition, she employs some well-trained therapists who operate the massage contracts she has with several major organizations and businesses around town. The collective income and some canny investments her dad made allows her to live in a pricey part of town. But it keeps her busy. I left messages at the apartment we're starting to share and at the school where she has her office. Then I took my plastic bag of old loot and went to my office.

The telephone rang right after I got there. It was a voice I recognized right off. "Ricardo."

"Hey Sean, how'd it go in White Bear Lake?"

"Pretty quiet apart from an encounter with some thug who tried to brain me with a piece of pipe."

"Yeah, I heard. Since you aren't talking to me from a hospital bed, I assume he was unsuccessful."

"I have a question or two. Here's the deal. I have some fragmentary evidence needing analysis."

"Is there a crime associated? This still the White Bear thing?"

"It is and I'm assuming there's a crime involved. I dug up a bunch of critter-shredded paper that could be currency. If there is a crime it's a pretty old one. The stuff I found was in the ground a long time."

"So I and White Bear PD don't have to worry about you meddling in some ongoing investigation. This is probably a cold case?"

"Nope and yes."

"Good. I think no one here or in White Bear is going to get bent out of shape until after you get some more answers. Let me know how it goes, and best to your lovely companion."

"Likewise."

I contemplated the plastic bag of booty resting on my table. For reasons I couldn't quite fathom, I opened the bag and dragged out some fragments to examine again. I snapped on some latex gloves. It bugged me, this sack of paper that was starting to stink up my office. I got out a magnifying glass and applied it to a scrap or two. That told me for sure that what I had was not play money, it was real. The quality was too fine. Even with an untrained eye, through the dirt and damage, I could see that. There was evidence that critters had attacked the bag from below, moles perhaps, and had likely dragged a lot of it away. Feathering their nests, you could say. The combination of water seeping down from above and animals attacking from all other sides had pretty much destroyed the bag and most of its contents.

I picked up a fragment of the canvas bag. It was once a heavy-duty bag; that much was clear. I poked around. Of the two dozen scraps of canvas, I could find only one that had any lettering on it. It was black and looked like it could be the tail of a formal "R." Not a lot of help at the moment. I couldn't even make a guess as to the original color of the canvas. Maybe it had originally been colorless.

I sifted through a few more of the paper scraps and quickly determined that all I was doing was turning the scraps into compost. As it dried, handling it broke it down still further. So I packed it all back in the plastic and turned to other aspects of the case.

I went to my computer and started searching. If you search the Internet with the key word money, you get a lot of interesting sites. Some are political, some cultural, some in the media. No help for me. I thought a moment and searched on paper money since I thought that's what I had. Could have been bonds, of course, or almost anything that required good-looking, elegant engraving. Maybe some of this had once been stock certificates.

Jackpot. There were even color pictures of bills. After an hour or so of perusing several sites I determined that I had indeed found the remains of paper money, old paper money. When I looked up at the window of my office, I detected that much time had flown and it was late in the day. So I packed up, locked up, called to leave another message for Catherine and went home through the summer heat.

5

It was early the next morning and already the summer sun was very hot. The temperature must have been pushing into the high eighties. I'd had a nice quiet early night in my own bed. It had been my plan, at six a.m. when I woke, to visit nearby Langton Lake. There is a paved path that circled both lobes of the lake. The path is surrounded by a tree and bush shelter belt which protects the area from nearby trucking terminals. Sounds slide through, but at least when the trees and bushes are fully leafed out one can make believe he is far from the industrial might of America. Except for the noises of big diesel engines and pallet trucks in the warehouses.

It was my habit to jog or slowly trot around the lake three or four times every week in the summer to keep the old bod in some sort of reasonable shape. Because I'm short, it's a more major undertaking for me than for some. I don't like to exercise in a crowd. My competitive juices don't run in that creek bed. So this morning, faced with rapidly elevating temperatures and humidity, I was about halfway around the lake already regretting my decision. I was sweating up a storm. I knew Spenser, that ex-boxer, wouldn't have minded. He seemed to run around the streets of Boston in all sorts of weather without ever getting winded. Mugged a few times, but never out of breath.

So I stopped and sank, panting, onto one of the green woven metal mesh benches the city had thoughtfully cemented to the ground along the path. Usually I would encounter a few fellow citizens of Roseville, or people from the nearby retirement home, or even those bright young people from the Christian college a few blocks the other way. But this particular morning the path was empty. Either they'd all paid attention to early weather reports, or more urgent business had called them away.

After a brief respite I rose and began again to wend my weary way along the path. My thoughts turned to my present case. The puzzle of my three oh-so-private Kavas was worth pursuing because I instinctively knew the adults' histories held clues to this case. The thing was, I wasn't hired to look into the family history. I was hired to get rid of the problems surrounding the puppy's finding of the loot. And the revolver. Mustn't forget the revolver. Already I had a sense this case was not going to have a clean outcome and I could hear Catherine's voice in my head, telling me to lay it all out for the Kava family.

There was no going back. I would get the money analyzed, hand over the rusty revolver to the law for some kind of analysis and when the information came back, assemble a report. After that, Kava would have to deal with the publicity and the authorities. I would collect my modest fee and bow out of it. I stumbled up my front steps and went to take a long cooling shower.

* * * *

Sitting on the deck on the back of my house in just my skivvies after a shower—the back yard is very private—I called a couple of local coin dealers, some of whom also deal in paper currency. One of them agreed to look at a sample or two of the scraps I had. I would visit him tomorrow. Now, however, I was going on a search for Kristi Kava's family.

In my basement I have a small office where I keep my secret stash of weapons and a desk and some old tax records, plus copies of current activity notes and reports. I have an old computer there as well. It's a little out of date and I'm only hooked to a dial-up line, but it gets the job done, eventually. At least it does if I don't tax it too heavily. My home office has important duplicate files, because I learned once that my regular office, the one with the address in the telephone books, is sometimes a target of violence and searches. This way, I can reconstruct records with a minimum of hassle.

The fact is, in this day and age, real privacy is pretty much a thing of the past. Anybody, particularly a somebody with an ulterior motive, can acquire all sorts of previously private information on you. And me. You can find explicit directions to almost any private address, including views of the roof of the address. All you need is patience and the right tools. I have both. I am, after all, a detective.

I started with my client's name, address and his occupation. Soon I had his social security number, his vital statistics, the record of a parking ticket in Forest Lake, and the date of his marriage. Soon there before me on the screen was one Kristi Polk, now the wife of Kent Kava. I knew when and where they were married, the birth date of their son, Alex, and I soon discovered that Kristi Polk had a secret. The secret might very well be the reason for all their reclusive behavior.

Kristi Polk had a social security number that was way younger than she was. Now, if you know the coding system, and that's not too hard to find out, social security numbers can tell you several things. What regional office issued the number and, with a fair degree of accuracy, when a particular number was issued. Stands to reason. They run in sequence out of each office. The higher the number, the later the number was issued.

For many years, the government has issued social security numbers pretty much at birth. So, the higher the number, the younger the citizen should be. There are exceptions. If you are a newly minted citizen, an immigrant, your number and your age will be out of whack. But there's another reason that an individual might have a new number. My mentor in the PI business and my experience told me that a person with a fresh new social security number was frequently associated with, or was what is sometimes now called, a person of interest. Kristi Polk was not a recent immigrant. What her number likely meant in this case was that she was in, or had been in, some sort of a witness protection program. I was about to find out.

I jumped off the Internet and called my friend at the Minneapolis cop shop. Wonder of wonders, he was at his desk. "Ricardo."

"Sean!" He responded.

"I need a favor."

"Uh huh. I seem to recall that we've had a conversation about this, about my not being your downtown clerk."

"I guess I'm up on the plus side of the ledger, my friend, but this might have to do with a sensitive area."

"Go on."

I need to check out a person, once possibly a person of interest, or maybe a former felon. I need to do it without revealing who or what are behind door A and without alerting who the keepers of Door A may happen to be."

"I see. This I assume relates to White Bear again and you want a very discreet probe by someone who really knows what he's doing. That would be me."

"Indeed it would. And it would also be someone who is discreet enough to stop immediately should you become alert to any official concern about your oh-so-discreet inquiries."

"That too would be me." Ricardo blew out his breath and said, "Who is the person of interest?"

"Kristi Kava, wife of Kent Kava, maiden name Polk."

There was a sort of pause. Ricardo was thinking, or maybe checking a list of current persons of interest. Or, maybe he'd dozed off.

"OK," he finally said, "give me an hour and I'll get back to you with whatever."

"Thank you, kind sir." We disconnected.

I spent the next hour rustling through my extensive and highly organized filing system. I looked in Bills Paid and discovered no surprises. Then I peered into Bills Due and found several pieces of paper, none of which appeared pressing, except for an undated note to call my lawyer. I did but he wasn't in the office. No surprise there. His answering service had no clue what he wanted me for. Maybe I had wanted him.

Then I looked in another folder, something called Invoices. My accountant said I had to have that. It's where I put copies of bills I send to clients. I don't have an elaborate bookkeeping system. In that folder I discovered that I am owed a couple of thou by various present and former clients. None of the bills was seriously overdue so I closed the drawer.

It was now precisely seventy-six minutes after I had last talked to Sergeant First Class Ricardo Simon. The telephone trilled and, wonders of wonders, it was he.

"For once, my friend," he said, "you do not seem to have fallen into a latrine."

"Charming."

Kristi Polk is the grand-daughter of a deceased Chicago gangster and ex-bank robber named Alphonse Patsy."

"Patsy? Really?" I was nonplussed. I'm not sure exactly what that word means but I was. "Grandfather. That means he was active in the 'twenties and 'thirties of the last century," said I.

"Right. Polk's father, Patsy's son, turned state's evidence, and sent his old man to jail. According to my source, the family was pretty bitter, but the son, whose name was Edgar, apparently looked around and saw all his relations in the crime business or jail, and didn't want the game. He'd just gotten married so he approached the state attorney general at around that time."

"I guess I can safely assume Edgar's family went into hiding with new names and help from state and or federal authorities."

"You are correct, and I can tell you also that Edgar and his wife, Susan, are deceased. They had only the one daughter, your Kristi Polk."

"Thank you very much, my friend."

"Raises a question, doesn't it?"

"Yeah, with that kind of background, how come the Kavas end up living in a place with buried treasure?"

"Let me know what you discover."

6

Almost as soon as I replaced the handset, the phone rang. The voice I'd been pining for whispered in my ear. Catherine was released from her managerial duties and she sounded delighted at my offer to squire her to dinner. We chose a small pasta bar not far from her apartment. I took a fast shower and pulled out a clean pair of red Keds from my stash in the spare bedroom. I wore a nice white combed cotton short-sleeved shirt and a pair of light-weight tan slacks. There was no way I could go heeled this evening. Even my recently acquired ankle holster would show. With or without the little .25 caliber revolver resting snugly in place. And why would you wear an empty ankle holster? I hadn't gotten used to the negligible weight of the thing so I was pretty sure I walked differently with the rig strapped on. I also knew Catherine would have smelled it, not that she went around sniffing my ankles.

Did I need a weapon? I almost never did. The daily life of most P.I.s is like mine, boring, mundane, ordinary. Spenser or Lew Archer to the contrary, we do not charge off randomly or otherwise, with any frequency, weapon in hand, to right the perceived wrongs of the world, despite what people read in detective fiction. Take Harry Bosch, for example. One exciting case after another, right? You only read about the exciting cases. Who'd want to read a whole novel about watching some dope trying to outwit his insurance company? Oh, sure, if the guy was a skydiver, or a whitewater rafter, maybe. But probably not. My life was more like that constable, whatsisname? Oh yeah, McIntire, in St. Adele up on the U. P.

By now I had driven across parts of several suburbs and wheeled into my assigned parking slot in Catherine's basement. I used to always park in the driveway, planning to just pop up to her door and then escort her to the car. But then, occasionally, we would have a drink, or some other distraction, like the time she met me at the door wrapped in one of those clear plastic sheets painters sometimes use. High heels, plastic sheet and nothing else. The building managers complained we were blocking traffic for too long too many times.

I might mention that when Catherine wears seriously high heels, she tops out at over six feet. That puts my nose, which was usually 55 inches off the floor, in an interesting location. Anyway, we now had a second leased parking slot in the garage below her building.

The restaurant a block off Lake Street was minutes away, and we were soon comfortably seated in a corner. I sat facing the room. I almost always sit with my back to a wall. Catherine found it amusing. I didn't mind. I'm aware of my idiosyncrasies, like almost always wearing red Keds with white soles. Except when I am seriously undercover.

"How are things at school?"

"Generally pretty much OK," Catherine said. "I lost three students today."

"Is that unusual? Three in one day?"

"Yes, especially in the middle of the term. No refunds." Catherine's massage school ran like most technical or academic schools, terms, tuitions and so forth. "The circumstances are a bit odd. All three are girls who started the same time last year. They live in the same neighborhood and pretty much hang out together. But these things happen. So, my friend, what's up with you?"

"I have this new client." I sipped my Pinot Grigio.

"A real case? One in which there is a real client who is not you? Paying for your services?"

"Affirmative." Catherine, a practical businesswoman, was always pleased when I had a real case for a paying client and wasn't running about waving a lance and practicing an imitation of Don Quixote.

"Can you talk about it?"

"I can." I often spoke with Catherine about my cases. I was careful not to violate client confidentiality, or put her at risk with sensitive information, but having no partner, or a secretary with great legs to bounce thoughts off, she was my insightful substitute sounding board. "A man who lives in White Bear Lake brought me an old rusty revolver and some very old money. The bills are useless as legal tender due to deterioration from having been buried for a very long time. Plus critters used the paper for nesting."

"Really old currency?"

"Yes, apparently issued around 1900 or before."

"Speculative guessing or expert opinion?"

"The scraps of bills I have look very old and they don't look like the money in my pants pocket. I plan to consult with an expert. Likewise the revolver is one that has not been readily available to hand gun buyers, except perhaps collectors, for maybe a century. It's in unworkable condition. Just possibly restorable to antique status."

"How old do you estimate?"

"Eighty to a hundred years for the pistol. That doesn't necessarily apply to the currency, of course, but it's my feeling at the moment that the cash is a mite older."

"Really. Nineteen oh oh or thereabouts, you said. How did this case come to you?"

"Man's son owns a small puppy. Spot, by name. One day Spot was digging in their back yard and unearthed a loaded revolver."

"Unearthed, you say."

"Yeah. Since the dog, Spot, belonged to son, Alex, father brought son and rusty revolver to me."

"They didn't call the cops? Odd, don't you think?"

"Very. Turns out they are an exceedingly quiet and private family. The man says he would rather work independently, even realizing he might make more with a larger construction firm. His wife, Kristi, works in St. Paul at some bank."

Catherine forked some pasta into her mouth and daintily wiped her lips. "Do you think the client or his family is more than innocent players in this case?"

"Astute," I smiled. "The wife, Kristi, may be somebody the cops call a person of interest. That could mean not necessarily a bad guy, exactly, but someone with strong ties to some sort of criminality. In her case, she has some criminal ancestors."

"And you know this how?"

"Research, my dear. No one is able to hide from a dedicated seeker of truth and justice such as myself."

"Well, seek out the truth of the bill for this dinner, my dear, and let's boogie."

We shortly found ourselves in Catherine's apartment watching the last blood red vestiges of the fading sunset while we enjoyed a small shot of some very good brandy and the immediate prospect of sleeping together in a large bed in the other room.

* * * *

The next day was Saturday. After a most satisfying night and even a rollicking start to the morning, I motored over to my simple office on Central in what is generally referred to as Northeast Minneapolis. Some people pronounce it "Nordeast." Those who do say it's out of their Scandinavian heritage.

My telephone answering machine showed no sign of being disturbed since I last examined it. I transferred a small amount of the rotting paper scraps I had dug up to a smaller plastic sack and went off to my appointment in a far suburb called Woodbury. There were no woods anywhere around. And as far as I had ever been able to determine, nothing buried, other than a few thousand tons of concrete used in foundation work. My destination was the small shop of a numismatist (I really like the way that word sounds—numismatist), a man who studied and collected coins and medals. This one was also qualified to discuss paper currency. I'd always believed that numismatist was a high-falutin' word for stamp collector. Turns out I was mistaken. So it goes.

"We differentiate our expertise between currency, coin and money," observed Alvin Jefferson. "I've studied it all. Some of us deal only in metal." He was a medium-built jolly appearing fellow with quick brown eyes that seemed to be constantly in motion and a perpetual smile fixed on his face. I'd expected an old man. I don't know why. Jefferson wasn't old, but he was well into his late forties or early fifties. His place of business was nothing special. It reminded me of a small jewelry store. There were some display cases on one wall opposite the south-facing windows. The cases held displays of medals—military, presentation, political, religious and so on.

There was no counter to separate the numismatist from the general public. But he had a deal table, four guest chairs and two hooded table lamps. One had a big magnifier attached.

He creased his forehead when I first opened my plastic bag in response to his, "Well, young fellow, let's see what we have here." We were immediately enveloped with the peculiar odor of long-buried paper which I'd first noticed when I got the stuff to my office.

"It's been in the ground a while."

I nodded. Jefferson poked at the scraps with a pair of tweezers. He screwed a jeweler's loupe into his right eye socket and examined a piece under one of the bright florescent table lights.

"Canadian. Probably issued around 1900." He picked up another scrap. "My, my, this, on the other hand, is U.S. currency. A private issue, I think. Hard to tell for sure, given the deterioration. But I'm pretty sure this was a bill from a bank in New York chartered by the government."

"They did that?"

Jefferson nodded. "Yep, authorized by the government and really pushed after the Civil War. 'Til then gold or silver was the most common exchange. But that stuff can be heavy, you know. Hard to transport in any quantity. The government authorized some banks to issue their own currency. Paper. Met with a lot of suspicion at first."

"So this stuff I have here is real?"

Jefferson looked pensive for a minute. "That's difficult to say. We'd need to look at a lot more. Do some analysis."

"What if it isn't real? Any way to tell for sure?"

He smiled. "Sure. There are tests for the authenticity of the paper and the ink. If you have a lot of it, chances are some is counterfeit. It's calculated that by the 1880s over sixty percent of the currency in circulation at the time was fake. Both the North and the South had counterfeiting operations going. Just like the Germans did during World War II."

"I read about that. Tried to ruin the enemy's economy."

"Correct. Now here's the thing. Assuming that's what you have. By the way, is there a lot of it?"

"Quite a bit," I said. I wasn't going to tell him how much. "It's all in pretty much the same condition as this sample."

Jefferson looked wistful. "That's too bad. Whatever you have that's real, if it could be put back together, could have significant value. Even if you don't have complete bills."

"Why is that?"

"First, all the currency issued by private banks, and that went on almost until the depression in 'twenty-nine, is still legit."

"Legit?"

"Right. Legal tender. In other words, you could spend it if you had it. I don't think a retailer would accept it, but a bank would."

"Interesting," I said. "What if I sat down and assembled some whole bills from these scraps?"

"You really only need fifty-one percent to claim the face value. Looking at this, it's probably not worth your time. However, should you find enough pieces to put together some bills, you might have something."

"Like what?"

"Here," Jefferson said, "look at this." He pulled over a fat catalogue and opened it. There were glossy pictures of bills of different denominations.

He pointed to a picture of one. It was a $5 dollar silver certificate dated 1896. "This one came out and then quickly disappeared. So it's relatively rare."

"Why is that?"

Jefferson smiled. "See the women? Winged Victory sort of depiction and her female supporters?"

"Yeah. Typical Greek or Roman statues, I suppose."

"Sure but it was determined that the women wore too little clothing and would bring psychological harm to American children clutching the bills in their grubby fingers."

"No kidding," I said.

"So they pulled the issue, making it rare and valuable."

On another page he showed me a reproduction of a bright orange $10,000 bill. He pointed to it.

"See this? Issued by a bank in San Francisco. Any bank in the land would give you ten grand for it. Face value."

I smiled. I figured a ten grand bank note issued in 1882 likely had even more going for it. I was right.

Jefferson smiled too and said, "But you wouldn't turn it in. It's a collector's item. You'd want to sell it through a shop like mine or maybe at auction."

"How much would it be worth that way?"

Jefferson looked at me and licked his lips. "Oh, on a bad day, maybe three hundred thousand."

I sat back abruptly. "Holy Toledo, Batman!

7

After I recovered my senses, I shoved the scraps of musty-smelling currency back into the plastic sack I was using. I stood up and looked at my consultant, Mr. Alvin Jefferson, ace numismatist. "I appreciate your time and expertise," I said, thrusting out my hand. Jefferson took it and stood up. "I'll appreciate it even more if you'll keep quiet about this interview and the scraps I showed you."

Jefferson smiled. "No problem. I deal with some pretty secretive folks in this business, so that's routine. Besides, you haven't told me much. I suppose you know where that money came from."

I looked at him. "I don't get you." I did in fact have a pretty good idea what he was getting at, but he surprised me.

Jefferson looked back, an amused flicker playing around his mouth. "Sure you do. I looked you up, Mr. Sean. You're a private investigator. I would think you want to know in the worst way where this buried currency came from."

He had me. Of course I did and I said so.

"There was a robbery in South St. Paul a few years back. In about 1930 or anyway the early thirties." Jefferson nodded sagely.

"Is that so? A few years back, you say."

"Yeah, a bunch of the boys robbed a railway express car when a train stopped here for a pickup. The government was cleaning up the currency flow and they were retiring a lot of privately issued bills, you know, stuff issued around the time of the Civil

War, getting a handle on counterfeit. Some smart fellas got wind of the shipment and knocked over the car when the train stopped in South St. Paul. Two railroad guards were killed when they objected. There was a shootout."

"Interesting. And I guess you figure this money I showed you is part of that swag?"

Jefferson nodded. "Yeah, I do. But you probably don't have all of it."

"You think?"

Jefferson smiled and said, "Over the years there's been a lot of rumors. See, two of the gang got nabbed within a week of the heist but they only had a small amount of the money."

"So you figure what I have here is the remains of the rest of it?"

"They got away with maybe a hundred thousand, according to the stories. Within a couple of years all the known gang was either killed or jailed. But a lot of the money just disappeared. Every so often some currency that might have been in that shipment turns up at an auction or somebody offers some bills for sale from that era. But nobody knows for sure exactly where the money that comes up for sale is from, you see. Point is that even the Fed admits that most of the cash from that robbery has never been found."

"Never recovered?" I found that hard to believe if all the robbers had been apprehended. "I suppose the money wasn't divvied up among the robbers so the bulk of the take was in the hands of a leader or two?"

"That's the story that's been around ever since I first heard about the robbery, back twenty years or so when I first came to Minnesota."

Jefferson showed me out and I took my smelly paper scraps in the plastic bag back to the office from where I called the South St. Paul police department. The other interesting piece of info Alvin Jefferson, numismatist, had imparted was that the robbery in question might have taken place even earlier, like maybe some time in the late 'twenties. Either he really didn't know, or he just wanted me to find out for myself.

The operator at the PD put me through to somebody, a detective named Tom McKinley. He was, he told me, in charge of South St. Paul's cold cases. The ones they hadn't turned over to the state. When I told him how cold my case was, he laughed and suggested I was pulling his chain. Then he explained after I explained what I wanted, that any records so old that might still exist were in storage somewhere.

"That doesn't sound very hopeful," I said.

"Yeah, well, I'll see what I can find. I'm sure we have something, because it's an open case. At least one guy was never identified and as you already know, Mr. Sean, most of the money was never recovered. Plus we lost an officer that day."

"In addition to the deaths of the two railroad guards?"

"Yeah, that's right."

"This old cold case seems to be closer to the top than first impressions led me to think."

"Yeah, well, as I say, it's on the board. Look, I'll try to find the file. Give me a few days and then call me again. OK?"

I agreed, thinking the detective was sort of waffling between interest and boredom. I hung up and decided to reach out to my person of interest, Kristi Kava.

The first time I called the house, there was no answer. I hadn't expected to reach Mrs. Kava, it was still too early and she wouldn't be home from the bank yet, but I did want to leave a message so she'd know I wanted to speak to her. I do that sometimes. Call before I show up. Sometimes it prepares and settles the target. Other times the target makes it difficult for me to reach him or her. Either way, their actions are a clue. People aren't always eager to talk to the law, even private law. Sometimes they want a lawyer present. Sometimes they are eager to talk, to protest their innocence. Other times they figure to try to outsmart me. As I say, any which way it's a clue.

I did a little office stuff and called again when the little hand was on six and the big hand was on nine. The male voice that answered didn't sound like Kent Kava, although I'd never talked to him on the phone. Phones are a crap shoot these days. I mean, there are a lot of good ones out there, but others, you wouldn't recognize your own mother's voice.

The other thing was, this guy sounded official.

"Yes. Kava residence. To whom am I speaking?"

Something was clearly off the meter. My alarm instincts sounded loudly in my head. "Uh, my name. Sure, my name is Ed Jones."

"Mr. Jones, I can't help you right now. I do want to talk to you. Give me a number where we can reach you."

Right. I hung up the phone and left the office. Something was going on in White Bear Lake and I'd better be there. So I went there.

Squad cars from several jurisdictions surrounded the house. There seemed to be a large number of higher-ups in evidence. I assumed White Bear was the primary so I found a cop in the right uniform at the yellow tape perimeter. He was assigned to traffic duty and scene security. I asked for my contact, assistant chief George Taft. I figured if this many cops were involved, the AC would be close by. The patrolman radioed somebody and then the patrolman nodded me inside the tape and pointed me toward a group of uniforms carrying a lot of gold braid. He didn't hold up the tape for me to duck under.

"Sean," barked Taft. The group split for me to enter. I was the shortest guy there by maybe ten inches.

"Can you tell me what's going on?" I said.

Taft scowled. "You can go in the front door. If you want to. But don't—"

"Yeah, I know the drill. Don't touch anything and don't get in the way." I walked toward the front door. Slowly. I really didn't want to go in there. It was obvious I wouldn't like whatever it was I saw. Turns out I was right.

In the small living room were two body bags. And a lot of blood spatter on the furniture. A BCA crime scene officer was crouched in one corner collecting evidence, I guess. "Ann," I said. She glanced over her shoulder at me and grimaced. "Sean. You know these people?"

"Who are they?"

"Kent and Kristi Kava, according to their IDs."

My stomach clenched. "Anybody else? A kid? Maybe a dog?"

"Nope. Just these two."

My stomach unclenched a little and I blew out a long breath.

Ann Hoover stood up and unkinked her knees. "I'm gettin' too old for this stuff. Their son Alex and his puppy are at relatives over in Little Canada."

"Anything you can tell me?"

"The house is trashed and there's a hole in the back yard by the garage wall."

"I dug that."

She raised her eyes and said, "You better find detective Jackson. It's his case, at least for now."

"Some question about that?"

"You notice all the brass in front? There's something about these people that's a little unusual. Even my boss is around somewhere."

I thanked her and went back out the front door and around the house. Somebody pointed out detective Stanley Jackson. He fit the name. He was big, blonde and Scandinavian right down to his slight accent. I would learn he was a savvy cop as well.

8

Walking back through the front screen door, the peculiar smell of blood and death gradually faded and I took several deep breaths to clear my head. I looked around the yard as I went deeper into the lot toward the garage. The sun seemed brighter, somehow, than when I arrived. The aroma of the bunch of day lilies in the corner was sharper, more penetrating. It was a good day to be alive. I wished the Kavas were alive to enjoy it.

I went to the garage. A Crime Scene guy knelt by my hole in the dirt next to the wall. "Find anything interesting?" Since I was inside the yellow tape he assumed I was official.

"Somebody dug a hole and filled it in again. Then sometime later, earlier today, I judge, that somebody dug up the loose soil and did some more digging."

"How do you know it was the same person who did both digs?"

The CSI shook his head and glanced at me. "I don't, it's early times. Say, do I know you?"

"I don't think so."

He squinted in my direction. "Wait a sec. Do you belong here?"

"Actually, I don't, officially. I'm a private investigator. I was working for the Kavas."

"Who?"

"The Kavas. The couple who…" I realized he had no idea who the dead people were. He was just there to process a crime scene. No personal involvement. Me, on the other hand, I seem to get personally involved all the damn time with clients and their cases. A strength and a failing, Catherine assures me.

"Have you talked to the detective in charge?" he said, still squinting at me.

"Briefly. I'll be filling him in."

"Uh-huh. I don't think I got your name."

"Sean Sean. Here's my card."

He reached out and took the piece of card, slipped it into the neck of his jumper. I looked down at the hole. It was much deeper and whoever had dug below my efforts had been a lot sloppier. There was a good bit of dirt thrown around on the lawn. Maybe he was in a hurry. Maybe he'd been digging after the murders were done. Or maybe he was trying to get the job done before the Kavas arrived home. Smacked of bad planning. Or, maybe the guy did his digging and didn't find what he was looking for. Maybe he waited for the Kavas to get home and then he tried to force information from the couple. What could they have told their killer?

A fairly obvious answer came to me as I went to the back door. They could have told the perp about the private detective—that would be me—who dug the original hole. They couldn't be looking for the money, could they? I was persuaded by my conversation with Al Jefferson that there wasn't a significant amount of cash that went into the hole. I mean, maybe twenty or thirty grand is all. Anybody with a modicum of sense would also know that the currency would have been picked over for the odd rare collector's bill.

That left the gat. That damned rusty revolver. The one still in my safe. I trotted up the steps and banged through the door into the kitchen. I hoped the Kavas hadn't died trying to protect me. "Where's Detective Jackson?"

"In here," he hollered from the front of the house. I went there. "I don't think there's anything I can do for you here," I said. "But I'll stay in touch."

"Yeah, I want to have a conversation with you, so be available. Tomorrow early."

I nodded. "I'll come out here. About eleven?" Jackson and I weren't acquainted and I didn't want any relationship with a cop to start out with a strain so I'd cooperate as much as possible. I went to my car and drove directly to my office. It was too late to take the weapon to the BCA, so I slid it into a paper bag and took it home to my little gun safe in my basement.

* * * *

"Look, Sean, I know you want analysis. You want me to get this piece into the system, get you analysis and a comprehensive report, and you want it all yesterday."

It was fifteen hours later. Sounds portentous, doesn't it? It was about ten the next morning and I was in the lobby of the snazzy new BCA central lab on the east side of St. Paul. Gone were the narrow corridors, made smaller by cartons of stuff piled along the walls. This place was airy, looked good and had some serious and intelligent art on the walls.

"Very good, Ann. You got it," I smiled.

"It just isn't going to happen. First, you are a civilian. There's no normal path for civilians bringing weapons here. Second, we're really jammed up, which is nothing new. Sheesh! I've got a boatload of cases in the pipeline. And look at this thing. It's old. We've got to remove this old ammo which could be unstable. There's not going to be any DNA. This weapon is a lost cause and tricky in the bargain."

I grinned. Ann flapped her hands when she talked, especially when she was excited. Her black eyes snapped and sparked and her dark ponytail bobbed up and down.

"Don't I pay taxes?"

Ann grinned. Then she laughed. Then she leaned over and bussed me on the cheek.

"I'm just trying to get things moving. I could have taken the revolver to the White Bear cops for processing then they'd bring it here to you. I'm just saving steps."

Her gaze sharpened. "What aren't you telling me? Is this related to something current?"

"Yeah, it is." Well, I was pretty sure it was. No absolute evidence for that, however. Just my experience and gut feeling. "There was a double murder yesterday in White Bear Lake. The detective in charge, Jackson is his name, will probably be in touch today if not sooner. I think the killer or killers were looking for this revolver. Why, I don't know yet."

More grumbling, but I could tell from the twinkle in her eyes she was going to take the weapon off my hands. I could have taken the thing directly to the detective, but I wanted to give myself a little space and not have to tell him just yet how it came into my possession. Was I protecting the boy, Alex Kava, or was I protecting myself? Probably both. Chain of custody was going to be a problem, of course, but I didn't think it would come to that. The revolver wasn't going to convict whoever killed the Kavas. But it might be a vital lead to the killer.

I'd looked at it long and hard before I turned it over to the Bureau of Criminal Apprehension. I made a few notes. It was a late nineteenth-century issue Navy Colt. I got that by doing a little Internet research and talking with a gun guy.

The weapon was rusty. It had four unfired shells in the cylinder and two empty casings. Maybe the slugs were in somebody somewhere. If so, it was a long dead circumstance. The one thing I knew for sure was that the revolver hadn't been fired in a lot of years. Which made things perplexing. The chances were that even if the guy who buried the weapon had used it to kill someone, he was most likely also deceased. So what was going on? I thought the weapon, the money and the burial might all be connected to the double murder of the Kavas in White Bear Lake. But why? Nobody was left alive who had anything to do with the buried stash. I was pissed. My client was dead and a kid I liked was parentless. Somebody was going to pay.

* * * *

At home I changed into shorts and an old U of Minnesota tee-shirt. I planned a forty-minute walk around Langton Lake, a relaxing drink on my deck, maybe a dip in my hot tub, and so to bed. So much for plans.

About two-thirds of the way around the lake there's an old stone structure. It's small and doesn't have a roof. One wall of large stones and rocks is mostly tumbled down. There's a heritage sign from the city that designates it as a historic site. The sign has a number but it doesn't tell you what the site is. You have to get a pamphlet from the city hall to find out. I figured the farmer who lived in the area before the coming of the Interstate and the truck terminals maybe built a smoke house. One day I'd have to go to city hall and get the pamphlet. But not today.

As I walked along on the paved path the city had thoughtfully provided a few years earlier, I heard a rustling noise. When I walk in the woods on this path, I often hear critters in the leaves disturbed by my passing. I heard birds and squirrels and other critters in my yard. But this was different. I knew it instantly, but can't say why I was alerted. Then I heard a sound that was definitely human. It was a kind of muffled cry.

I turned off the path and peered into the squarish stone structure. A small, very dirty, face was turned up toward me. There were smudges on both cheeks and something that might have been a blood smear on her chin. The expression in the eyes was one of extreme fear. I smiled and squatted down. "Hi there," I said softly. I smiled again. I used my warmest tone, the one I reserve for telling a client I've screwed up and the target is lost to us. The small creature snuffled and let the snot running from her nose drip down over her mouth. I'm not sure how I knew the urchin was female. My detective instincts, I guess. I resisted the urge to wipe her face. Eventually I must have telegraphed my need because she took her own swipe at her face with a grubby hand. It didn't help much. Mostly it smeared the mucus across her cheek.

"Are you lost?" I said. "Is your mommy or your daddy around here somewhere?"

In response she shook her head of dark tangled curls.

"I don't wanna go back," she whispered

I didn't have a clue where "back" was and it was pretty clear she couldn't tell me. A breeze rattled through the trees and I flinched. Ever since I'd found the urchin my senses had been on high alert, though I'd been at pains to try to appear as calm and unthreatening as possible. Then I remembered the clean handkerchief I'd stuck in my hip pocket as I left the house. I pulled it out and offered it to the girl. She looked at it but she didn't take it. She shrank back into the rocky corner as if she was trying to fuse herself to the rough stone wall. I had a sense if I tried to get any closer, or wipe her nose, she'd scream. I stood up.

She screamed.

Then she covered her eyes and screamed again. The birds were stilled. Critters twitching through dry leaves were frozen in mid-twitch. For a moment I thought the trucks in the nearby lot had stopped running as well. This tyke had a hefty pair of lungs on her. Maybe she'd been practicing. I surveyed the immediate area hoping a parent or someone who knew the kid would materialize. No such luck. After a couple more screeches, the child subsided into a series of hiccups interspersed with some off-key sobs. I slowly squatted down again.

We weren't getting anywhere this way, but she did finally take the handkerchief from my extended fingers. "OK, look, my dear, we have to get going. The sun is going down and it's going to get

chillier. I can't leave you here, so let's move out. Do you understand?"

She looked at me fearfully, or so I interpreted her brown-eyed
gaze. I steeled myself for what was to come, wishing for the first
time in memory that I had a cell phone handy. I stood up half-way
and reached out a hand to her.

Surprise. She sort of struggled to her feet and in the process,
took my slender fingers in her chubby ones. I stepped back a pace
and gently tugged her toward me. She whimpered and then I saw
she was barefoot. The stones had cut her feet and there was dried
blood on her skin from scratches on her feet and ankles. Nuts.

I leaned closer and wrapped my arms around her and hoisted
her up into my arms. I made cooing noises to her. Wonder of wonders, she giggled and burped and ran her smelly arms around my
neck in a hard clutch. Moving steadily and carefully so as not to
alarm her, I shifted her body to a more comfortable place against
my shoulder. I cooed some more, gently patted her back and we
began the long walk back to civilization. Her arms around my
neck did not slacken. We'd only got about half-way home when I
realized my new little friend had fallen asleep.

I passed a few people on the path, some of whom ignored me.
A few stared. I wasn't sure what they might be thinking. I didn't
look much different from a thousand other suburban dads, carrying their kid back home. Why I was on a path a long way from any
homes, with a small child and no vehicle for her to ride in was a
question. What's more the kid looked pretty grubby and even ne-
glected. So I got a few hard looks, but no confrontations. People
don't want to get involved.

I didn't want any hassles, but what if I was a kidnapper? What
if I was a separated parent stealing my own kid from her mother?
If that, why would I be wandering around a lake in the weeds, so to
say? So, unlikely that this isn't my kid, and said kid isn't screaming. But it bothered me that the passersby raised not a single ques-

tion. Somehow, there has to be a way for people to be assured that things that appear suspicious are looked into. So I got home without being busted, carried the kid into the house and found a blanket. I put the child, still asleep, on my sofa and went to call Roseville PD. Then I got a washcloth in some warm water and washed her face and hands. She woke up during the process so I offered her a glass of water. I didn't have any milk. She wasn't thirsty, or maybe she didn't like St. Paul water.

The squad that arrived an hour later carried a Roseville cop I knew named Sergeant Lasker and her partner. Lasker smiled and said, "You'll be a hero, Sean, at least to Maria's parents."

"Maria what?"

"Ridder. She lives in Shoreview. Her sister was supposed to be watching her this afternoon while her mother went shopping. Seems the sister brought her to that ball field behind the retirement home and lost sight of her just long enough so the kid wandered away."

"So, what happens now?

"We'll return her to her mother who will probably punish the kid's sister for losing her."

Lasker bundled the little girl into a blanket and they left.

9

I called Detective Stan Jackson of the White Bear Lake Police Department and confirmed our meeting at the Kava's home the next morning. Since I no longer had a paying client, I figured I would be completely truthful, open and honest with the White Bear Lake homicide investigator. Right.

I drove up the short driveway beside the house, which was already starting to look a little forlorn. I wasn't sure why it should look that way. Maybe it was just me. Detective Jackson was standing beside the garage. I parked behind his car and walked over. He nodded as I approached and said, "This is where you found it, right?"

"To be precise, that's where Spot found it. The revolver."

"Right," Jackson said. "The dog Spot. I had a conversation with the boy, Alex. You want to tell me the rest?"

So I did. I explained how I had first met the Kavas and what I had done with the weapon. Then I told him about the money.

"Where's the money now?

"It's in the trunk of my car," I said. "I figured to turn it over to you since I no longer have a client and this is a murder case."

"Yeah, no billable hours in this one," he said. Right then I began to dislike this detective. Making that kind of assumption could be dangerous. Innocent people were occasionally sent away to nasty places like prisons because somebody made an assumption and didn't look carefully enough at the evidence.

"Well, detective, you think what you like about me, but I want to have a conversation with Alex, if there are no objections."

"Unless the relatives who have him object, I don't care."

"Did Alex tell you about their visitors?"

"Why don't you," said Jackson. He pulled out his notebook.

So I did. I related what Kent Kava had told me about the parade of visitors who had shown some interest in his garage renovation project. Unhealthy interest, in retrospect. Then I mentioned the guy I had apprehended.

"You have a person of interest to this case locked up," I said.

"We do?"

"Yeah, a minor felon who attacked me on Tuesday. Name of Harlan Ford?"

"Oh, him. He's out on bail."

"That's interesting. Who got him out?"

Jackson screwed up his face in thought. "I can't exactly remember, except it was a pretty high powered defense lawyer from Minneapolis."

"Did this lawyer come out here personally?

Jackson shook his head. "No, he sent one of his young minions. It was just a simple assault, after all."

"I think it can be argued that length of gas pipe is a deadly weapon."

Jackson shrugged.

"It's suspicious that Mr. Ford is out on bail when the Kavas are murdered. By the way, how were they killed?"

Jackson thought about my question while we walked the few steps to the back of my car. "Shotgun. Each got two loads."

"Jesus." I was sorry I'd asked. "Find the weapon?" I opened my trunk and indicated the dark green double-strength trash bag therein. It was nested among the usual crap one often finds in car trunks; a spare tire and spilled dirt from when I carried some special soil from a garden shop to Catherine's apartment. There were some old tools, that'd been there for years, maybe since I bought the car. I was not a tool person, except when really pressed. There was also a snake of jumper cables partially under the trash bag. Every Minnesota car has to have a set of jumper cables. It gets really cold here sometimes.

"The killer took the weapon away. So, that's the stuff you dug out of that hole over there?"

"Right. A lot of old money."

"You asked an expert, right?"

I nodded. "Yes, a man named Alan Jefferson."

"Yeah, he called us after he saw a story about the murders. You must have told him something."

"I must have." I'd think about that a little. Was I getting careless?

Jackson leaned in to the trunk and untied the top of the bag. "Whew."

"Yeah, it smells, doesn't it? From all those critters for all those years."

"You think this was from some local heist?"

The man was starting to use my language. "Dunno, detective. It's obvious the stuff has been in the ground a long time. So this is no recent robbery. I haven't had much luck yet finding new information, but I plan on some serious searching in a day or two. And there is one other thing." I figured he'd get a heads up from the BCA as soon as they ran tests on the revolver and I wanted this detective on my side as much as possible, so I was being forthcoming and cooperative, I was even trying my hand at charming. I didn't know if it was working, but I was giving it my best shot. Catherine would have been proud.

"I told you yesterday about the kid and his father coming to me right? Well they brought me the pistol. An old Navy Colt revolver. I took it to the BCA and tagged it to this case. You should be hearing from them in a week or so."

"So it's a really old revolver?"

"Yeah, one they stopped manufacturing just after the turn of the century. The twentieth century, that is."

Jackson scribbled another note and said, "Anything else you care to tell me?"

I shook my head. "I don't think so, but I will stay in touch with you. I don't suppose you have an address for Mr. Ford?"

Jackson shook his head and stuffed his notebook back into his shirt pocket. "Nope. Call the office. I'll let them know you're working on this with us. But let's be clear here. I don't want you getting in the way of this investigation."

The interview had gone OK and I'd given him everything I knew. Unlike a lot of cops he also wanted to know what I thought.

"Just tell me this." He was mildly pissed that I'd taken the rusty revolver to the BCA. "Why did you withhold the revolver? You must have known that we'd find out about it."

"Look, Detective," I'd said. "There's no law a citizen can't deposit something with the BCA. It's a rare occurrence, I know, and there's no assurance the weapon has anything to do with anything, right?"

"I think you should let the professionals decide that."

"I know it hurts you to admit it, but I am a professional and so are the BCA folks. And here's the thing. Because I, a civilian, took the weapon to the BCA, you can talk about it in places you otherwise wouldn't be able to."

Jackson stared at me for a moment then a sly grin surfaced. "I get it. You'd like word to get around that the weapon found by a citizen's dog in the back yard of the site of a double murder is being processed by the BCA."

I nodded.

He chuckled. "Could be dangerous."

On that nice note we parted company. He was talking on his cell phone and walking across the yard toward the back door of the Kava residence as I backed out onto the street and headed west, podner, west to my Minneapolis office. I had a lot to think about. I was still cogitating when I unlocked and walked in to hear my honey's voice on my answering machine just hanging up. So of course, I called her back immediately.

"Are we still on for dinner?" I asked when she picked up.

"If you show up at a reasonable hour."

"Count on it."

We disconnected and I contemplated my navel. That wasn't a real thing. In my youth, we accused contemporaries who were too self-centered of being navel gazers. It was meant to be derogatory. In this case I was in what I recognized as a disturbed state. I was bereft of clients at the moment, due to the untimely deaths of Kent and Kristi. Did I do something to cause these murders, in even a peripheral way? What was going to happen to the boy? What about Spot, the dog? I made a note to check with the people who now were taking care of Alex Kava. I needed, mostly for my own peace of mind, to find out more about his circumstances and the people who now sheltered him.

Then there was the felon in the wind. Where was Harlan Ford? And what was his connection? I was going to find him if the cops didn't net him first. When I got to Mr. Ford we were going to have an intense face to face. I didn't believe for a minute his appearance on the White Bear scene was mere happenstance. Somebody sent him there. But who and why? It had started with Kava's project to renovate his garage. I reviewed my memory and my notes.

Kava had told me people came around weeks before the dog found the revolver in that hole. There were those two guys who tried to talk their way into the Kava home, again, weeks before the money was discovered. Apart from the normal city staff who would have routine concerns, there seemed to have been a much higher level of interest among the citizenry in general. Why? Maybe, if I could get a handle on that, I'd find a path to the murderer who left a twelve-year-old boy parentless. I locked up and went to Kenwood where I discovered that Catherine had changed our plans. The lights in the apartment were low and there was soft music on the stereo. This lovely female person met me at the door with a nicely prepared gin and tonic, and a long, heartfelt kiss. She handed me my drink and leaned over to wind her smooth arm around my neck.

"Sit there." She placed me on my preferred end of the sofa and knelt before me. I still had the glass to my face so I missed her move.

"Whoa, here. What's going on?" By now she had my shoes off and her agile and educated fingers were plying their craft on the heel and instep of my left foot. I tell you it felt wonderful and it wasn't more than a few minutes before her ministrations had their effect and most of the stresses of my day faded into the background. Other than a complete full-body massage, there's nothing like a foot massage to set you right once again. I bet Kay Scarpetta would have felt a lot lower levels of angst and anger about her niece and assorted other troublemakers if she'd had a good foot massage every couple of days.

Needless to say, dinner and the rest of the evening, extending on through the night followed the same sensual and sensuous path. By morning we were both satisfied and more than ready to face the vicissitudes of our lives.

"Are you going to talk to that poor boy, Alex Kava?" Catherine was almost dressed, whereas I was being something of a slug-a-bed and had only managed to shower, shave and struggle into my skivvies.

"Yeah, I'm afraid I am. I know the cops have talked to him already. I just hope they handled him carefully. This Jackson I mentioned seems to be a reasonable sort."

"Ramsey County has a good child protection service," Catherine said, slipping a nice tailored linen jacket over her shoulders. I shrugged into my usual summer outfit of belted slacks, a short-sleeved white shirt, a Twins blue-billed baseball cap, and my soft llama-skin ankle holster. My socks were gold-toe black cotton nylon blends inside my red white-soled high top Keds. Before I put my shoes on I minutely examined the soles for cracks, seriously worn spots and other imperfections, like errant wads of gum.

I caught a questioning look from Catherine when I strapped on the holster. "I don't seriously think I'll need it today, but I want to get more comfortable carrying it. I still think I walk differently than when I'm not wearing it."

"I think you're overly sensitive. As I've told you at least twice, I can't see a difference. You still have that adorable swagger. On the other hand, or foot, I'm more than perfectly happy when you don't find it necessary to wear one of your weapons." She floated out of the room on her long delectable legs and I followed, like an obedient puppy. I tried very hard not to swagger, but the fact is we are a couple who are both well aware of our several talents and we see no reason to be overly modest, particularly in our private lives. It was one of the nice things about our relationship.

10

I sat at my desk swinging my feet. I hadn't put the small wooden box in the right place. Since I was alone, it made no difference. I had to have my desk chair cranked up to its highest point so that my chin doesn't rest on the desk when I work. But that meant I couldn't quite reach the floor with my feet. I wasn't heeled, hence the box. My ankle holster was empty because I'd stashed the weapon in my safe. I wondered idly if that's where the phrase "heeled," meaning carrying iron, a gat or a gun, actually came from. Doubtful.

I had just got off the phone with the gatekeeper for young Alex Kava. With great reluctance his aunt in Little Canada had agreed to let me talk to the boy. There were several restrictions. I could live with them but I was going to have to be careful. I wanted to get everything the boy could tell me, and I only had forty-five minutes in which to do it. Explaining to Aunt Susan that the boy might tell me significant stuff that would save his life and solve the murder of his parents seemed to cut very little ice with her. Her focus seemed to be totally on protecting her nephew.

I was cool with that.

I leapt into my car and sped off to Little Canada. Another northern suburb of the saintly city. At least it was in the general direction of Big Canada, north of our borders, although there was little I could see to justify its name. It was an old town, one of the oldest in Minnesota, settled by French Canadians, apparently, hence the name. Never mind. Twenty minutes and I was parked in a white gravel driveway in danger of being overwhelmed with ambitious weeds. The house was old, white clapboard siding in need of a paint job. There was a screened porch across the front. I dislike screened porches. Too many bad things can hide there— mice, spiders, errant birds, like that. Maybe another Harlan Ford.

I went through the screen door and, seeing no bell buzzer, I banged the flat of my hand on the wooden front door. It was a heavy paneled affair with an elaborately etched floral pattern in the single glass that effectively obscured a clear look at anyone standing on either side of the door. It made me a little nervous. There was no response, so I hit the door again. I listened, then I heard approaching footsteps. I stepped back, no need to get into Aunt Susan's face right off the bat.

The door opened and there she was. A blank look. I think she had carefully wiped all emotions off her face.

"Yes?" She said. "Can I help you?"

She was taller than I, but most people are. "Good morning," I said. "I'm Sean Sean. We spoke on the telephone." She looked to be in her early fifties. A well-put-together individual.

The woman peered down at me over half-frame reading glasses. She wore a gold chain around her neck and attached at each end to the black bows of the glasses. I'd bet they were cheap plastic magnifiers she bought at the local Walgreens. She folded her arms under an impressive bosom and stared at me.

"You're a lot shorter than I expected. Identification, please." Polite but firm. Good, I thought. A hand reddened by years of work shot out toward my chin. I fished my P.I. license and my driver's license out of my wallet and handed them up. Her fingers curled around the plastic and she drew back her hand. Her fingernails were short and ragged and I noticed that the cuticles needed work. Hers was the hand of a woman who did some kind of physical labor. I'd bet she had a garden behind the house. Her hair was in a loose bun and she wore a looser University of Minnesota sweat-shirt and worn jeans that were stained but clean.

She stared at the pieces of plastic I had given her. Then she glanced at my face, comparing the picture with reality, I guess. I thought it was a lost cause; I mean, whose driver's license picture looks like the owner? Then she nodded and said, "All right, you can come in." Her bosom rose and fell in a mighty sigh and she preceded me into the dim interior hall.

I closed the door and we paraded down the hall that bisected the home. Interesting cooking odors tickled my nose as we passed the door to the kitchen. The last room was a sort of family room between the kitchen and the back wall of the house. It was a big room stretching across the entire width of the place except for the corner where a door probably led to the back steps and out of doors. Two walls were of glass from waist to ceiling and the sun flooded in, brightening everything. There were a couple of divans, some overstuffed easy chairs, a table or two and lots of books and boxes of games. At the card table in the middle of the room sat young Alex and on the floor at his feet, Spot the dog. Both looked up at me when we entered the room. One of them wagged his stubby tail.

I went to Alex and nodded, reaching to shake his small hand. He took my hand and smiled at me. "You're the detective. Mr. Sean, right?"

"That's right. I'm glad you remember me, Alex."

His aunt had come to stand beside me, looking down at her nephew. The change in her was remarkable. Love and concern radiated from her face like a force. I relaxed. Nothing and no one was going to harm this boy any more if she had anything to say about it.

"Are you going to find who hurt my mom and dad?"

I nodded, still holding his soft hand. "Alex, I'm going to do everything I can to find whoever it was who did those bad things.

That's why I'm here. I just have a few questions."

"A policeman was here already. I didn't like him much."

I sat down on a stool across from Alex and leaned my elbows on the table. He was working on a big jigsaw puzzle. I couldn't make out the picture, but when I looked down there in front of me was a piece that obviously fit a gap in the edge. Alex was working on getting the edges done first, exactly the same as my preferred procedure. I picked up the piece and put it in place. Alex grinned and said, "He can help me with the puzzle, Aunt Susan."

"Looks like it," she said. "Can I get you some coffee, or a soda, Mr. Sean?"

"A diet Coke or Pepsi would be great," I said. I had apparently passed her test because all the limits and strictures faded away. Two hours and a fabulous ham sandwich later, Alex and I had completed about half the puzzle and I had answers to all of my current questions.

"Alex," I said. "I have to run along now. You've been very helpful. If it's okay with your Aunt Susan maybe I can come and see you again. What do you think about that?"

Aunt Susan looked as if she wouldn't mind and Alex nodded his golden head enthusiastically. "We can save the puzzle until then, maybe."

"Well, that would be nice, but I can't tell exactly when I can come back, so you and your aunt better finish it. We can do another one next time, perhaps." I stood and stretched. Aunt Susan saw me to the front door.

"I assume Alex will be going back to school soon. He needs to be protected."

Susan nodded. "I wasn't listening close, but I could tell he gave you some important information."

"He did."

"The policeman has some of it, but you learned more than they did, I think."

"I'll be in touch with them. Thanks for the lunch."

"Thanks for coming. You were good with him. Ever been a teacher?"

I shook my head, her hand, and went to my car. Driving home I thought about what Alex had told me. Especially that some of the men who had come around had been "creepy." A couple of them in particular had bothered his parents. He remembered pieces of conversation at the dinner table. His mother had speculated that one of the men who had shown up had been connected somehow to her family's past. That bothered me more than I let on to Alex. He was also pretty sure there had been more people hanging around, especially after Spot had dug up the revolver. Somebody who said he was from some state inspection agency had come around. Alex had a remarkable memory for some things. This particular individual had apparently showed up on a Saturday morning when his father was not at home.

Alex had been with his mother at the door and I was able to elicit an impression that the man was pushy, insistent and had upset his mom. But Alex couldn't give me much of a description except he was big and smelled like he smoked. When I'd asked the boy if the man was black or white, he'd just looked blank. He really didn't know. Which didn't mean much. It probably meant the man's skin was similar in color to his own. So what I had was fragmentary, but it was a Hell of a lot more than I'd had when the day started. It was pretty obvious that somebody badly wanted to know if anything significant had been dug up around that garage and what it was. What I thought was that it wasn't the money. What I thought was that it was the pistol. That damn revolver. It must connect someone to something that was important today. I was going to figure it out if it killed someone.

11

I didn't start with the weapon. Even though I knew instinctively the gat was a key to finding the murderer, I needed to work up to it, pursue lines of inquiry that would eventually come back to the rusty revolver.

So after I checked the office answering machine, I drove to the library. I might have gone down the hall to the Revlon cousins, who could make computers do everything except bake bread, but they had informed me that a vacation to the south of France was on their immediate schedule and the office was closed for two weeks, a time segment we were in the middle of at the moment.

In the library I looked up money, currency, official coin of the realm. And I discovered some interesting information. First I looked up the robbery itself mentioned by the numismatist. A book called "Dillinger Slept Here," by some guy named Maccabee, told about the robbery, which actually happened in 1933. Then I learned a little more about the money.

Most of the time the people who manufactured our money used green and black ink. There were a few special bills like the gold ones and sometimes bills came in different sizes at different times. Some of them were really rare, like the five that Jefferson had told me about so collectors thirsted after them and they garnered high prices.

Well, what can I say? That didn't matter because none of the paper I had recovered would ever be redeemable or even positively identified. Of that I was quite confident. Probably.

I also did a little reading about the weapon Spot the dog had found. It didn't take long to confirm its identity. The markings on the weapon I had already written down indicated it was a Colt revolver, the one called the Navy Colt. It had been manufactured and issued to both Army and Navy personnel for years between about 1892 and 1901. The serial number was missing and I remembered it looked to have been crudely chiseled off, just like in those old B movies my ma used to take me to at the neighborhood theater when I was a kid. The book told me more than 100,000 had been manufactured. So it wouldn't have been hard for the skells that did the robbery to lay hands on one.

I learned that the weapon was most likely a military issue even though there was a civilian version. The one Spot dug up had lanyard swivel points, which were not put on the civilian model. I guess in the fog of war, the military wanted its people to hang on to their armament. But I wondered who among the robber gang might have been in the military.

I reshelved the reference book where I'd found it and went looking for more grist for my mill.

I didn't think the revolver's make and model would be of much help; criminals who use such weapons tend to be opportunists, grabbing whichever weapons are handy. I figured that the pistol was evidence that whoever buried the loot had intended to return shortly for the stash. The weapon hadn't been protected from weather in any way. But no carbon dating here. The pistol had been in the ground for a long time, a fact supported by the condition of the money. I was sure money and gun had been buried at the same time and that time was early in the twentieth century.

I looked up Kristi Kava and what I found was interesting. First off, it was a little surprising that she was even in the electronic card catalogue. Well, her family was, anyway. Turns out Kristi Kava was a Polk. Now most people wouldn't have a clue about that, but if you're in the PI business and you have contacts with law enforcement in the Twin Cities, especially if they are generally good relations, you sometimes break bread with various acquaintances who are professionals in the business. And cops tell stories, war stories we call 'em. Pretty much every profession has them.

I twigged to Mrs. Kava's birth name, Polk. It was a name I recognized, thanks to a couple of cops, a little John Barleycorn, and a crime historian named Paul Maccabee. Polk, you see, was the name of one of the gunmen who was believed to have participated in the robbery of the railway express car in South St. Paul back in 1933. That's the one in which a bunch of thugs killed two railroad guards, and a local cop, and scampered with a big bundle of swag, including, it now seemed likely, the trashed cash I had dug up next to the deceased Kava's garage. Of course, it could be a different, unrelated, Polk.

I went to a pay phone in the library and called the South St. Paul cop shop. When I was connected with detective first class Tom McKinley, I said, "This is Sean Sean, the detective? I'd like to sit down and discuss a fella named Byron Polk."

A sigh. "All right. I sort of expected you'd be calling me."

"This afternoon?"

So it was arranged and right around three I was directed to a second floor conference room in the South St. Paul police station. Two men stood close together talking when I walked in.

The man who turned to greet me was older, a white man nearing retirement with what I took to be the weary look of a cop who had seen too much and experienced too much in his long career. He was in his shirtsleeves, white, tie snugged up to a buttoned collar. He was taller than I—who isn't—and he didn't look at all rumpled. His name, he said in a voice that sounded like too many late-night, stake-out cigarettes and old coffee, was Tom McKinley and I couldn't tell whether he was pleased to see me or not. He introduced the other, younger man as Sam Monroe, another homicide detective. Monroe and I nodded at each other and he left.

"Siddown, Mr. Sean," said McKinley. "You want some coffee or water?"

"Just water'll be fine."

He sank back into the heavy wooden chair at the end of the table and I sat right around the corner of the big table. He placed one big hand on a sizeable stack of file folders. They were mostly yellowish, a little grimy, and some of them had tattered corners. All of them looked well used.

McKinley looked at me for a moment and of course I looked back. It wasn't exactly like a couple of roosters looking for territorial advantage or pecking order superiority but it was close. Finally he said, "Okay. After you called I talked to a friend of yours in Minneapolis, Rich Simon?"

"Ricardo. Yes, we've known each other for a number of years."

"This is the case file on that robbery. Nineteen thirty-three it was. Summer. Three dead officers and the street pretty well shot up. Damn Tommy guns throw a lot of lead."

"I read Maccabee. He got it right, I take it."

"He did. But we are pretty sure there was another guy involved. And we think he was a local guy, related to this woman in the White Bear Lake case."

"Kristi Kava, born Polk," I muttered.

"Right. I spent two days skimming this stuff after the word got around about finding the stash of old money in White Bear Lake to get up to speed with the facts. I'm gonna let you go through this stuff, although you can't take anything out and I really don't want to make any copies. So you should write down anything you want to remember." He stopped and looked questioningly at me.

"Works for me. But first why don't you tell me what you know and what you think."

McKinley looked mildly surprised and then the planes of his face relaxed and I got a definite feeling that he was softening, starting to think of us as closer to a collaboration. And that was a good thing. I wanted his perspective on the old case.

"It was in July that year. The department knew the railroad was bringing a car stuffed with old money through town and we expected a shipment of old paper from the Federal Reserve in Minneapolis to come here by truck. But the truck was delayed so it wasn't part of this." McKinley shuffled a copy of a newspaper over to me. It had big headlines and a photo that showed a street scene with a couple of people and a single car parked at the curb.

"I've got a map in here but this is the street where the thugs rolled up and just started shooting. In the service I would have called it suppressing fire. Made everybody keep their heads down.

"Meanwhile, across the street and half a block down another vehicle rolls up to the train siding where the Railway Express and their guards are waiting. More shooting and the two guards are killed. They never had a chance. One guy jumps out of the truck into the railroad car and starts tossing out those canvas bags they used to use, you've seen 'em?"

I nodded. Only in pictures, but I knew what he meant.

McKinley took a swig of coffee—he'd forgotten my water—and went on. "Four, maybe five bags of the cash. Then the first car with the rest of the gang rolls up. The truck made a U-turn and they took off down the street heading south on Concord. About that time, a rookie cop named Ed Washington runs into the street from around the corner. He has his gun out and probably shouted for them to stop. They gunned him down."

"So I count seven guys in the gang—four in the car and three in the truck. What happened to them?"

"All of them were later killed or went to prison for various other crimes. Except two guys."

"Polk? And the unnamed?" I asked.

McKinley smiled, mirthlessly, as they sometimes put it. "Him. Here's another picture you'll want to see." He slid out of the topmost file a smudged 8x10 glossy. This one showed a man in a fedora standing spraddle-legged in the back of the truck with a pistol upraised in one hand. It must have been snapped only moments after the robbers began to roar out of town. The angle was from high and behind.

"Pretty lucky shot."

McKinley nodded, and I examined the photograph. The vehicles were heading away from the photographer so there was no hope of identifying the man. The enlargement didn't show the gang's other vehicle, which I assumed was somewhere ahead of the truck. But it did show a crumpled figure in a dark uniform lying in the street close to the right front fender of the fleeing truck; the cop, Eddie Washington.

I peered more closely at the pistol in the gangster's hand. From his stance, it appeared to me the weapon was raised just as it would have from the recoil. Especially if the gunman had not had his arm in a locked position. I glanced up at McKinley.

He nodded. "Washington had some shotgun pellets in him and he was hit by at least one bullet from somebody's Tommy gun, but the shot that killed him was a .38 caliber lead slug."

"Can you have this blown up so we can see the pistol better?"

"Already done, and after you started nosing around in this case, I had the blow-up digitally enhanced." He slid another picture onto the table in front of me. This one showed the right hand, a piece of his shoulder, and the pistol with what might have been a wisp of smoke at the end of the barrel. "Our weapons guy swears that's a Model nineteen-oh-one Navy Colt, military issue."

"Thirty-eight caliber?" I asked, already sure of the answer.

"Yep. I'm lead-pipe certain that's the gun that killed Officer Eddie Washington moments after the robbery went down."

"Any other photographs?"

McKinley shook his head. "None that we know of and the photographer is long dead. I don't even know what he was doing on the roof of the building where he was when the robbery happened."

Tom McKinley and I looked at other pieces of paper in the files. Most of the information dealt with reports by various officials who had been involved over the years in the on-again, off-again investigation. Notes on the captures and sometimes the deaths of known members of the gang were included.

What I noticed after an hour of skimming reports was that the thug named Polk had never been apprehended and there was one name always missing. I looked at McKinley. "It looks to me like they never identified the seventh gang member and this guy, Polk, was never pinched."

McKinley smirked at my use of old jargon and nodded his agreement. "That's why the money you found up in White Bear Lake is interesting to us. It ties directly to this case."

"Too bad the money is in such bad condition."

"Is it?"

I stared at McKinley. "Either you think I filched some of the supposedly restorable cash I found in the hole, or what?"

"Here's the thing, Sean. As soon as the story arrived about the money dug up by that garage, various people put their eyes on this file. And I was told not to worry about it until the Chief brought it to me and sort of ordered me to sit on it. So now I've made a few people angry because I wouldn't let them at it, except when I was present."

"Seems as though things are stirred up a bit," I said. "Another thing is this. As soon as Kent Kava started working on his garage and got a permit from the city, people started coming around."

"People."

"Yeah, inordinate interest was being shown toward a simple private renovation project. From that I deduce that somebody knew something about the place, and the money and the pistol buried in the hole seem a logical choice."

"I get it," McKinley said. "Something to follow up on. Anyway, Polk was a criminal with local ties. He had family that mostly worked in the stockyards. He didn't care for hard labor, apparently. He was never apprehended at anything illegal, and there are rumors about that. How'd he always seem to be absent when raids happened, for example."

"Expected, under the circumstances."

McKinley agreed. "Right. It's assumed Polk and the unidentified guy ended up with the bulk of the money. It's also assumed that Polk and the unsub, as we call 'em now, retired from their criminal ways. Of course, we don't know about the unidentified, he could have been killed or jailed and never linked to this crime."

I looked at him. "What do you think happened to him? The robber who was never identified?"

Detective McKinley considered my question. He looked at the table. His right hand twitched and smoothed the file folder under his fingers. Then he tugged on one ear lobe and looked up. I watched his eyes track across the ceiling and then down to the big windows and out at some unseen view.

"Detective," I said gently, "you do understand the question, right?"

He sighed and nodded. "Oh, yeah, I understand it all right. I was afraid this would come up. See, this is the question that's dogged this case since the beginning. For all these years. Mostly it's been buried like that money you dug up. It's like this file is one big shoe and everybody's been waiting for the other one to drop."

"And I'm the other shoe. Or at least, I'm maybe pushing that shoe off somebody's toes. Is that it?"

"Yeah."

"Okay, maybe I can make it a little easier. Here's what I think. Fact of the matter is, we're having a conversation that pretty much confirms what I've already figured out about this case. I think that Kristi Polk Kava is related to your Mr. Byron Polk, and maybe to the unidentified gunman who was sitting in the truck cab when the guy in the back shot the cop."

I leaned forward and stabbed a finger on the photograph to emphasize my point. "I'm betting this guy is Polk. What's more, I'll lay odds the guy in the truck, the one whose face never shows, is somebody in this town. Or maybe his relative is somebody.

"I'll lay even more money that most of you people here have a pretty good idea who he is. Am I right?"

McKinley shrugged and looked miserable.

"But you probably don't have enough to arrest the toad. Even now."

"Right on all counts. There's one more thing." He took a deep breath. "Officer Eddie Washington? He was my uncle."

12

Now I knew I was in it. This case was exploding in all directions. The whole thing was wound too tight and was as incestuous as all get out. I wanted to ask McKinley why he'd been assigned to baby-sit this particular case but I sensed it wasn't the right time. Maybe there'd never be a right time.

McKinley shrugged as if he was readjusting his entire psyche and all his muscles at the same time. "We're done here. Let's get a drink," he said. "I'll tell you the whole stinking story."

Ah, maybe some enlightenment was coming.

He gathered the files together and stood up. I had more questions, but they'd have to wait, and see what else I learned. McKinley was going to proceed in his fashion, not mine. So I shuffled my notes together and shoved them into my inside pocket. McKinley dropped the files in his office and we went out and across the street in the waning afternoon sun. I realized as we paused on the pavement to let a car pass by that I was standing very close to where the train heist had started. The part of the gang that had been assigned to keep the cops away had been parked across this street in that alley, maybe twenty yards from me. It gave me a funny feeling.

"That's right," McKinley said, eyeing me, "we're standing right where it happened, seventy-some years ago."

We went into the saloon where my guide was hailed by a small group of men standing at one end of the bar.

They were all cops and they welcomed McKinley like a lost fraternity brother, which of course he was. Me, they allowed into the circle but I could tell it was only because I was with McKinley and their easy conversation over the beers they held and the popcorn or peanuts they tossed in their mouths shifted to topics a little less intimate.

McKinley explained briefly what I was all about and I, briefly, described the Kava murder scene. "Detective Stanley Jackson is the man in charge," I mentioned. There was no reaction. Either they didn't know the man, which was possible, or they were being cautious with an outsider.

Time, as they say, passed. We snacked. We drank. It had become obvious McKinley wasn't quite ready to tell me "the whole stinkin' story." I drained another beer, shook hands with the detective and started toward the exit. McKinley stopped me and said he'd be leaving as well. I stood at the saloon door and waited for him. Then we exited the place side by side and headed back across the street toward the cop shop parking lot. The sun had left the sky and the streetlights cast an unhealthy orange glow over everything but it was still pretty light. We were three steps into the empty street when two quick snaps rang out and something plucked at my sleeve. McKinley grunted and went down in a heap. I dropped on top of him, instinctively scanning the street for any movement. There was none.

"Gun!" I screamed. "Shots fired! Officer down!" I probably screamed some other words. I don't remember.

Cops and civilians appeared from different directions some with weapons. The door to the saloon behind us exploded outward as our drinking companions poured into the street. I looked at McKinley and swore. He was lying partly on his side with one leg drawn up and facing away from me. A dark spot appeared on his white shirt just to the left of his shoulder bone. I grabbed his head and turned it toward me, feeling for the carotid artery. He had no pulse. He was dead. I swore again and looked at the men crowded around. My hands started to tremble. All cops, friends or acquaintances of the dead cop. All with guns in their hands.

There was a suspended moment in which sound and motion seemed to stall. Then more pandemonium. The detectives and the uniforms fanned out, searching, peering through the bad street lighting for any sign of the assailant. I remember hoping they didn't encounter any civilians carrying weapons or making threatening movements. More uniforms poured from the cop shop in front of us and I heard the siren of an ambulance.

A big uniform appeared in front of my face. It had a lot of brass on it. The captain wearing the uniform peered at me. "You must be the PI working that old case? Sean Sean?"

I allowed as how that was me.

"You hurt? Let's have a paramedic check you over." He took me by the shoulder and we stood up. "See anything? Like where the shot came from?"

"No, but look at McKinley. The shot must have come from over there." I pointed. There were already four uniforms and some others trotting in that direction. The captain waved his arm and pointed. Three more uniforms left us and went to back up the group already fanning out. There were calls and an occasional shout from different directions, but very quickly the scene resolved itself. Whoever had fired the fatal shots was gone. Or he had secreted himself in plain sight.

The big captain handed me over to a paramedic who sat me down on the back ledge of their bus and began to look me over. Questions, more questions. No, I hadn't been shot, hadn't seen anything, yes the shots must have come from behind me. There was a ragged tear in my right sleeve right over the bicep. I stuck a finger in it and remembered there were two sounds. Two shots. I shrugged off the EMT and stood up. One of the detectives who had been in the bar was standing, head down, over McKinley's now-covered body. They wouldn't move him until the investigators had processed the scene. I was willing to bet the detective wouldn't leave either.

I looked at him as I walked up. He appeared to be younger than the deceased. "Excuse me. Detective?" I said.

He raised his head. "Sean?" I nodded.

"I want to tell you something. It may help."

He took a deep breath. "Tom was my mentor and later my partner. We go back a lot of years. My name's Monroe. Sam Monroe."

I nodded. "I remember. Listen, Detective Monroe, there were two shots, very close together. One missed, it went between us. I can give you almost an exact position where I was standing."

His bright eyes lasered into mine. His mouth was a grim, almost lipless slash across his face. "Let's see it."

We went to the door of the saloon and I pulled it open enough so I could step inside. I let the door go, turned and pushed it open to the street, then walked across the sidewalk at the same rate we had done a few minutes earlier. A crime scene tech watched. I stepped off the curb and made two steps to McKinley's body.

"Here," I said. "Right here. I felt a pluck at my sleeve, heard two snaps and McKinley went down. I grabbed at him and went down with him."

I started to sink down beside the body but the tech stopped me. "Just stand there for a mo," he said and took a couple of pictures. Then he took some more from reverse angles. "Good deal. This will help a lot to lead us to the shooter's position and maybe we'll find the other slug." He turned and went back across the street. Monroe shook my hand.

"Thanks, man, much obliged for your help. We'll be talking in the next day or so."

I checked with the officer in charge and got my walking papers, so I left. I was in no doubt the shooter had tried to take out both of us. And since there was only one thing that linked us, the Railway Express train robbery in 1933, I was willing to bet a lot of money I didn't have that the South St. Paul robbery was directly linked to Kristi Kava and my bag of ruined cash. And that Navy Colt revolver.

13

I decided to go to Minneapolis, instead of home to Roseville, driving through the edge of South St. Paul toward the freeway. It was farther, but the atmosphere was bound to be friendlier and a lot more inviting. Catherine was waiting at the door with a drink for me when I got there—I had stopped for gas and called her before I got to her part of Minneapolis called Kenwood. The single malt scotch went down easy and fast. Normally, I think of good single malt as a sipping whiskey, but at this moment I needed the alcohol. I don't make a habit of hard or heavy drinking like some P.I.s I could name but won't. Mike Hammer, for example. I find it gets in the way of clear thinking.

Catherine just looked at me silently as she handed me my second drink. "What?" I said. "Do I detect a little disapproval here?"

"Not really. It's just unusual to see you belt down good scotch that way."

"Come sit here," I patted the couch beside me and she did. "I have had a bad afternoon. The culmination of which was getting shot at and damn near killed." I went on to explain the day's events. She sat very still through my recitation, a sign of both worry and calculation.

"You know, there's a job opening at the school coming up this fall."

"Is that a fact. Would this be an overture?"

"It would certainly be safer than what you do now," she said.

Although she didn't nag, this was something we had discussed before. Catherine worried about me, something that I of course both liked and was concerned about. Long term worry by one partner about the other can lead to a parting of the ways. I knew that from observation, even though I rarely did divorce work.

"What sort of position is it?" Maybe if we talked about it, and my qualifications, we'd get away for a while, from a consideration of my present occupation.

"My general manager is leaving in the fall. George is moving to San Francisco."

"George has a nice title," said I in my most neutral tone of voice, "but isn't he basically an office manager?"

"Yes, my darling, but he has other responsibilities. And with the right person in the job, I'd be willing, even eager, to give up some of my supervisory activities. Eager, I say." She dimpled at me.

"You mean personnel oversight, building security, payroll management, and so on."

"Correct," she said.

"I do have experience with those sorts of responsibilities."

"I know." Now she was blowing in my ear.

"Not vast, but a certain level of familiarity." That's one of the side benefits of being a P.I. If you do the kind of self-effacing undercover work I do, sometimes involving probing employee activities to root out fraud and theft and other illegalities, you get to work in a variety of jobs. Along the way I had picked up numerous basic skills and a wide if elemental understanding of office jobs, a few of which I was even adept at. But they wouldn't be my choice for a new career. None of them. Far from it. I wasn't really, seriously, interested in a career change, was I?

"This offer, it is certainly something to think about, and I appreciate your even considering me." I was pretty sure I knew what her shark of a CPA would say about this. Her managers would take one look at my resume, laugh loudly and tell Catherine how she was being seven kinds of fool and that the business would shortly be in the dumper; all in a quiet and polite voice, of course. "Meanwhile, I have this knotty little problem to deal with."

"Yes, you do. I have been thinking about it. This time, I'll run through the scenario and you tell me what's missing, or where I'm off track."

"In the end," Catherine finished, "it all comes down to the revolver." She was hanging up her dress while I watched from our bed. It was two hours later and we had decided bed was the right venue in which to conclude a rehash of the case. "I think Kristi Kava and the revolver are the two keys. She and the weapon are somehow tied together."

"Also my conclusion."

"What you have to do is find that connection. I'll bet it's a family thing."

"You mean that the revolver was used in the great train robbery, possibly even to kill patrolman Washington and maybe in some other illegal activity."

Catherine turned and looked at me. "But not after the robbery. Because we're pretty sure revolver and cash were buried at the same time, yes?"

I hesitated. "That's been my assumption all along. And it's a pretty good one. On the other hand, I guess it's possible the weapon was buried later. I don't know how we check that, but if it was, even a day or two later, we might have to consider that it was used by or against someone in something very touchy. The other aspect is links to Kristi Kava. I will not be surprised to learn that somewhere in her family lies a ticking bomb."

"To coin a phrase," said Catherine. "Plus, you wouldn't want to forget about her husband's family."

I stretched, seeing a long dim road of complications stretching ahead. "Forget it, at least for now. Let's turn out the lights, you climb into this large comfortable bed and we'll set all aside until tomorrow." And so we did.

* * * *

The next morning, it being a Thursday, I called my friend Ann at the BCA. Although she was a DNA expert, not into firearms, she knew what she knew and she also knew how to acquire facts she didn't know. Sometimes just walking into the next office cubicle and asking a question can provide one with great gouts of valuable information.

"Sean, that's really hard. There are some ways to get clues as to a time frame, but it seems that trying to determine the length of time a piece of steel has been in the ground depends on a lot of variables, like its condition at the time of burial, its protection. I mean, was it well conditioned at the instant of burial? Was it already a little rusty? Circumstances like that. We have some idea that the piece you found was probably in the ground with the chewed up cash a very long time. I think you can assume with high probability that the Navy Colt was buried at the same time as the cash. I would hazard a guess, based on your description, that whoever buried the money and the pistol expected to return for both within a day or two. A week at the most. After that there might have been enough rust to make it inoperable. Frozen hammer, for example. At that time, it probably could have been renovated, but much later..." I could almost see her expressive shrug.

"Yup. I didn't find any evidence that the revolver had been greased, or even wrapped to keep it dry. 'Course the boy could have lost all that when he found it," I said.

"The lab hasn't found any indication of any wrapping or oil, nothing," Ann said.

"If I take the heist as a starting date, assume the guy with this relatively small share of the loot from the train robbery was a minor member of the gang, I might be able to pin down why he never came back for the stuff, and thus who he was."

""How would you do that?" she asked.

"I'd look at arrest records in the local area for people who might have been associated with known members of the gang."

"But what if this alleged gangster left the area?"

"Then I'm screwed, to put it delicately. But I don't think that happened and here's why. There have now been three killings since the pistol was recovered. Both the Kavas and Detective McKinley in South St. Paul."

"Yeah," Ann interposed, I heard about that. Bad business. Glad you weren't hit. Why do you think the shooting of that cop is connected to your case?"

"I am pretty sure the shooter was either aiming to take me out or get both of us. That means there's something about the case and the recent discovery of that pistol that threatens somebody's comfort level big time. McKinley and I are only connected through the train robbery case and likewise with Kristi Kava."

"Not Mr. Kava?"

"I don't think so. I think Kristi and her husband bought that place in part because she or somebody in her family knew the money and pistol might be located somewhere on the property. I have information that they paid a bit over the evaluated price, and they made an offer only two days after it came on the market."

"Have you talked with the sellers?"

"Not yet, but that's on my agenda."

"Interesting reasoning. Sean, I gotta go. My machines and several prosecutors are waiting. Stay in touch. Oh, the pistol would never have operated after the boy found it without total disembowelment and replacement of some parts. The ammo was likewise inert. Naturally there is no evidence such as fingerprints or anything else associated with the weapon that might remotely be labeled evidence. 'Bye."

I made an effort to do the kind of search I told Ann I would do. I called several departments where I had contacts. With the help of certain computer whizzes, I even accessed the BCA database of old cases around the time frame in question. I found a data entry for patrolman Eddie Washington listed as an open but cold case. Nothing that I found seemed to tie to either the known gang members or to an active thug not known to be in my particular gang. It stood to reason, that these guys would not have had a newbie along on something as big as this train robbery. I turned my attention to the Kava family. It was time to have another talk with Alex Kava.

14

This time Susan Polk had no hesitation about letting me see the boy. She even had fresh coffee waiting. I took a roundabout way to get to their location, constantly checking my rearview mirror and the cross streets. I was taking no chances. Three deaths in one case unsettled me to the max. I wasn't sure the boy could identify anyone directly, but he might have some useful information buried in the recesses of his mind, knowledge of which even he was unaware. What I hoped was that I could winkle it out of him—winkle, a word from across the pond—without his being aware of the importance of what he might tell me. Because of the murder of Detective McKinley, I didn't want to lead the enemy to him. Careful as she was being, Aunt Susan would be no match for a stone killer with a Glock or a Mac 10.

When I arrived at the aunt's domicile in Little Canada I decided to park across the street and down two houses. I wasn't tailed, I was sure of that, but surveillance can be a chancy thing. I didn't want to lead anyone to the boy's location.

This neighborhood made a permanent watch almost impossible. A stranger hanging around would be quickly noticed. Neat homes, set back not too far from the street. Low plantings close to the buildings, nothing big enough for one to skulk behind and listen in at open windows. No curbs or gutters and no sidewalks. Across the street I saw two neighbors talking, standing by idle lawnmowers. That was another thing. The houses were all well kept with permanent plastic siding or fresh paint. I didn't care which, you understand, but these were all clues to a neighborhood that paid attention to whatever was going on around them. Hell of a difficult place for a self-respecting PI to survey somebody. Then there were the blue and white Neighborhood Watch signs.

So I parked, trotted across the street at an angle and up the front steps. Mrs. Polk was waiting for me at the door. Mrs. Polk, I had learned after my first visit, was a long-time widow who knew how to live alone and like it. She had a no-nonsense personality and I had already sensed she was exactly right for her nephew, Alex, in these circumstances.

"Why didn't you park in the driveway?" she asked, motioning me to precede her into the hall and back toward the kitchen. I could smell the coffee.

"Basic precaution," was all I told her. I didn't want to alarm the woman needlessly, did I? It was going to be a delicate conversation after I talked with Alex. I still had to be sure the boy and his aunt stayed safe. But how much protection were they going to need?

"Hey, Mr. Sean. How you?"

The boy stood up from the couch where he'd been fooling with an IPod.

We shook hands and I sat in an easy chair across from him so I could watch his eyes. I had no reason to think Alex might lie or be evasive, it was just habit. "I only have a couple of questions this morning."

Mrs. Polk handed me a cup of black coffee and retreated to another part of the house, another measure of her trust. I hoped I was worthy. I was also relieved because I was still considering how I might shield her from any information I got out of Alex. The fewer people who knew the kinds of questions I was asking, the safer Alex and his aunt were likely to be. He grinned up at me, relaxed, waiting.

"Alex," I said, after we'd explored his past school day. He was in summer school, attending a few classes, mostly to give him some activities so he wouldn't spend too much time brooding about his lost parents. It also helped him keep up with his grade in school. My impression was he was resilient and reverting to his basically sunny personality. He smiled a lot and didn't fidget. After a few minutes his eyes started to wander toward the back door. I knew his dog was out there.

"I want you to think about the time when your dad was starting to clear out the old garage. Can you do that?"

He nodded and I could see this was bringing up some sadness.

"Your dad told me some people started coming around to ask about his plans. Do you remember that?"

"Sure. Some of them were sorta rude."

"Rude, how?"

"Well, they were pushy, like they thought they had some sort of right to ask all kinds of personal questions. That's what my mom said once."

"Those are the ones I'm particularly interested in. Do you remember any of their names?" Alex looked down at his bare knees and seemed to be trying to remember. He looked away and then he looked down again. He squirmed on the chair. He wanted to help, I could see that, but he didn't know much.

I recalled the man from the water company who had dropped by when I was digging by the garage. I described him in a few (I don't mind saying) deft phrases. But Alex shook his head. Blank memory, apparently. "What about the man who wanted to look around inside your home? Do you remember him at all?"

Alex looked up and smiled. "Sure. My dad got ticked at him. But there were two guys—men that time. They were there together. One was real tall, and the other was shorter. He looked mean."

"Were they fat? Or thin? Can you remember anything about the way they dressed?"

"The short one smelled bad."

"Really? How?"

"I asked Dad if he smoked. My dad said yes. They both wore suits, I think. They were sort of normal, you know? But there was one black man who came alone. He said he worked for the city inspector. I think that was a different day. He was big."

I smiled at the boy. He was so earnestly trying to help. Even though we didn't mention his parent's deaths, he knew I was a good guy and he wanted to help me find his folks' killers.

"Define big," I said.

Alex frowned. "Define?"

"Yeah, you know, was he bigger than your wagon? Smaller than a Volkswagen? How big was he?"

A grin. "O.K. He was the tallest man I have ever seen, I guess. He was taller than Aunt Susan. His skin was really dark, almost black, and he had dark hair in funny rows."

"Very good, Alex," I enthused.

And so it went. After several minutes it was clear Alex was getting tired of trying to remember the people who had come by. He began to fidget. So I quit asking him questions about adults. Instead I took an array of pictures out of an envelope I was carrying. Alex had been eyeing the envelope ever since I'd showed up, but he was too polite to ask about it.

I laid a bunch of photographs on the table in front of him. "Alex, I'd like you to look at these pictures. Tell me if you recognize anybody."

He stared down at them, pushed them around with his fingers. Finally he said, "Him. I saw him. He came to our house, I think."

He picked out two others. One was Detective Stanley Jackson, the cop handling the shootings; the other I knew to be a building inspector for the city of White Bear Lake. The third was a mug shot of Harlan Ford, the thug I'd encountered in the Kavas back yard. Alex couldn't recall exactly when Ford had first appeared but he was certain it was before Spot had dug up the revolver and the cash. That seemed to indicate that whoever was behind this mess had foreknowledge. Ford. He was a person of interest.

For a few more minutes we talked about his puppy which was in the fenced back yard. He wanted me to go with him to see the dog, so we went to the back door. I stayed inside and Alex ran out into the yard. I watched him for several moments. He seemed happy, adjusting, but I wasn't. My heart still ached for him. Susan Polk appeared and called Alex in to get ready for lunch.

"Mrs. Polk, let me ask you this. Did either Kent or Kristi ever mention to you anyone in particular who came around asking about the garage project? Anybody they thought was more obnoxious than usual?"

She thought about it for the few seconds it took for us to reach the front door and shook her head. "I'm sorry. Although we saw each other in family gatherings, you have to understand, the family was never close. I didn't even attend Kristi's wedding. It's a little ironic that now I have care of her son."

I opened the door to the back yard and got Alex's attention. "I have to go, Alex," I called. He glanced at me and waved. I waved back and turned away. Susan Polk put her hand on my arm as I went toward the front door. "Mr. Sean, I understand the police may think these murders are the work of some thieves or are just random acts of violence. Don't you believe it. I have no information about them, but I am as sure as I can be that Kristi and Kent were killed because of a family connection."

I looked at her with a question in my eyes.

"There are a lot of good Polk people, but like most families there are some bad ones as well. You go looking for those, Mr. Sean. If you need some money, well, I have a little savings, you know." With that she nodded once and shut the door firmly behind me. I paused, my eyes tracking right and left along the quiet street. It had cost Susan Polk a lot to say that.

Self, I said as I went across the street to my car, a lead, if not an outright clue. I would hie myself to an Internet terminal and see what more dirt I could dig up on this Polk family. I also began to think seriously about the logistics of some sort of protection for Susan and the boy. If the Polk links were criminous, and people of influence thought the boy had some incriminating knowledge, these two could require protection.

* * * *

It turned out not to be so easy. The Roseville library was between Susan Polk's place and my own home, so back I went. One terminal at the end of the row was available, but there was very little information about the Polk family of Minnesota. At least, there was little that seemed to be relevant in any way. Now I'm used to digging up all kinds of stuff on people. Research. It's sort of akin to what novelists do, I'm told. They collect a monster quantity of information but they only use a very small amount of it in the actual project or book.

It turned out there were several Polks in the Twin Cities area in the 'twenties, but the family name grew scarcer and scarcer as the years crawled by. Small families, movement out of town, like that. I made a few notes. There did seem to be some criminal connections, all in the mid to late 'twenties, but they were indistinct and I knew that time and distance had only made them less useful. After winnowing down census and other information, I identified four possible links. The most immediately accessible connection appeared to be a guy named Raymond Polk. He would have been the right age in 1932, and he'd lived in a rooming house in St. Paul Park.

Then I called Detective Jackson, the man in charge of the case in White Bear and explained that I thought a loose surveillance on the kid and his aunt would be a good idea. He agreed and said he'd arrange something.

I drove to St. Paul Park, a southern suburb. The highway took me through the construction along Highway 61 and I found the address. I had no particular reason to visit the place. It's hard to explain exactly why I sometimes do things like that. I knew the buildings would have changed and there wasn't any chance of learning something useful. But I went there anyway.

According to city directories, in the 1930s the street had been a row of boarding houses. Today it was an aging commercial district, but well kept and active, judging by the number of cars parked on both sides of the street and the number of people on the sidewalks. I could just see the dark waters of the Mississippi River a few blocks farther on to the west. The address where Raymond Polk had lived had morphed into a dry cleaning establishment, some years ago, from the look of the place. It was now part of a national chain. I got out of my Taurus and walked down the block to the corner. I looked around and stared at the business for a few minutes standing in the hot sun. I stared at the upper, private floors, wondering what sort of people lived there now. Then I got back in my car and drove the twelve miles home along the hot highways. Somewhere on that route I grabbed a hamburger and a malt.

15

I looked out the front door at my sun-washed street. I'd been in the basement since early morning cleaning my arsenal and generally wasting time while I thought about what Alex had told me. Maybe I could track down the White Bear building inspector. And maybe I could get a lead on the two pushy bad-smelling guys who had annoyed Alex's mother. Now it was getting on towards noon and I figured I better stir my stumps, as somebody used to say.

First though, it was off to my Minneapolis office to see what the mail might have brought in. It had been two days and the room was probably packed with checks and offers of employment and who knew what other goodies the postal guy had brought? Right.

Wonder of wonders there were two checks for past services rendered. There was also a bill from my lawyer. He'd been unsuccessful in a little matter of property damage. It seemed my insurance company took umbrage—there's a good word, umbrage—at my running a car into the corner of this man's garage. Not my car, you understand. Wasn't my garage either.

I'd been playing tag with a young fellow who thought he could out-maneuver me on the city alleys after his buddy robbed a convenience store I was watching. I'd managed to latch on to them when they skidded into this alley in North Minneapolis. I guess the driver panicked when I bumped his rear end at about fifty miles per. He fishtailed a couple of times and I caught him just right about halfway down the block. I tapped his bumper once more and by the time he got it stopped, his car had taken out half of one side of some citizen's garage. Unintended consequences. I mean here I was, trying to help clean up the neighborhood, wasn't I? Crumley's Milodragovitch never got that reaction from folks down in Texas, did he?

The citizen who owned the garage was screaming at me, the cop who showed up was being hollered at by the kid in the driver's seat, and I was trying to keep the kid who had done the actual holdup from hurting himself with the pistol he was waving about. Eventually he was taken off to jail and things cooled off. My attorney Bernie had to deal with the insurance companies. It all worked out after everybody calmed down and they didn't even raise my rates.

So I wrote a check and went looking for the fellow in White Bear Lake's code enforcement office. His name turned out to be Sam Pierce. He was tall, very black and he'd worked for the city for a dozen years. He was a pleasant fellow and he wore his hair in tidy corn rows. He remembered meeting young Alex Kava. We had a nice chat and he told me the two cigarette-smoking individuals who had acted a little boorish, if Alex was to be believed, didn't and hadn't worked for White Bear Lake in any capacity whatever.

So I could cross that possible lead off my list. On to St. Paul. Now everybody who has ever heard of St. Paul probably knows about James J. Hill, the empire builder and about F. Scott Fitzgerald and the swells who built Summit Avenue and all the fine mansions along that street that runs almost straight as an arrow from the big cathedral on the hill right down to the river bank some seven miles distant. But not many people from outside the city know about the little warren of streets that cling to the steep bluffs just below mansion row. You don't have to be a mountain goat to navigate them, even in winter, but it helps. So I drove down to the curve where Summit hauls off to the left when you are heading toward the capitol building. Right there is a big brick and stucco pile called the University Club. It's not on University Avenue. Why it's named the University Club I don't know. You'd have to ask the founders and they're all dead.

The place has meeting rooms, a dining room, a sort of a bar or club downstairs, a pool and other stuff, including a library. Catherine has taken me there a couple of times to readings by poets she likes. Anyway, if you turn left and follow Summit, you get to the political center of the state, but if you go straight, you find yourself roaring down a very steep hill called Ramsey, named for the first governor of Minnesota Territory. Alexander Ramsey his name was. Partway down the hill is an alley which, if you hang a sharp left turn you can enter and soon find yourself on a narrow street that runs along the side of the bluff to a switchback a long city block away. There are garages for the big houses up top on the left side and clinging to the down slope are houses. One of them is the rooming house with the address I was looking for.

It was a nicely kept rooming house and it had eight mailboxes hanging on the front wall beside the front door. The door was more ornate than you would expect on a place like this. There was only one doorbell. So that told me the place was a rooming house and not an apartment building. I rang. At least I assumed I did. No sound was detectable to my listening ears. I rang again and there was a rumbling sound from somewhere inside. Eventually the door opened on smooth quiet hinges.

"Yeah?" mumbled the apparition that appeared before me. To suggest he was large would be insufficient. He must have weighed three hundred pounds or more. He was clad, if that's the right word, in a pair of blue overalls. They looked new, unfaded, but not exactly clean. His beard was long and scraggly medium brown and I was pretty sure I could see bits of stuff caught in the curly strands of hair that surrounded his mouth and hung to the middle of his chest.

"I'm looking for Raymond Polk."

"Yeah? So'm I. He's late on his rent and he ain't been around for a couple of days now. I'm thinkin' 'bout cleaning out his room."

"Can I have a look-see while you do that?"

"Naw. They's laws about that. An' don't be waving no saw-buck at me. I read all them books. You got a card, I'll call you if he shows up."

So I handed over my card. He took it in two grubby fingers and let loose a huge breath of fetid air that made me dizzy for a few seconds.

I walked off the porch, taking deep breaths to clear my system of whatever nasty germs might have been floating around the guy. I have few illusions any more. It would be a long time, if ever, before that guy called me, besides which I figured Polk might have flown the coop. There were still a couple of other Polk addresses I could visit, one of which sat on what my map told me was a bluff looking east at the Mississippi, over what at one time had been the massive South St. Paul stockyards. I drove up the meandering city streets until I reached the bluff, not far from the small South St. Paul airport.

The street was a dead end and only two blocks long, finishing its work at a heavy steel barrier attached to four massive timbers set into the stony soil. Beyond the barrier was a whole lot of space. There was no turnaround, and there were only two houses on the last block, one on each side of the street. Both were set in the midst of large swales of lawn bushes and trees. The house on the inside, not directly on the bluff itself, was the address I sought.

To say the place was going to seed would be accurate. Maybe even mild. It was a large two story wood frame building, essentially a cube, at least the sides appeared to be the same dimensions as the front wall. There was a big open wrap-around porch with a railing of fat lathe-turned posts. Traditional spirea masked the open lattice work below the porch floor that faced the street and the neighboring yard. I stared at the upper floors because I could see dormer windows open. There were curtains in each window, hanging limp in the humidity and still air. No light showed behind the glass that would betray the outline of a watcher. The reflections in the glass rippled like old glass would. The window frames were wood. None that I could see on the front of the house had ever been replaced with aluminum or vinyl. The frames were dark and in need of paint. The lap siding looked as if the previous century had gone by and nary a brush of paint had ever touched those virgin surfaces.

The ridgepole that held up the attic roof and the shingles was as straight as the sidewalk sagged. Quite a contrast. I picked my way up the walk to the wide front steps. They too had seen better days, probably fifty years ago. I was almost afraid to mount them. That's what you do, you mount steps, or staircases. Better than mounting horses, in my view. I'd done that and I didn't like it much.

I confronted the massive front door, wooden, of course, with an elaborate glass panel with beveled corners that threw prismatic beams at me. A fussy figured white cloth curtain with elaborate open work designs backed the glass.

Somebody, I read, when discussing some of the differences between male and female writers of detective fiction, remarked that she could always tell if it was a woman writer because males never noticed the curtains or the drapes.

Hogwash. I notice such things all the time, if only because windows with curtains can conceal people harboring evil intent. Being alert helps keep me out of harm's way. So I stepped to one side as I raised the brass knocker suspended in the middle of the door and let it smash down on the dented and scarred brass plate. The window pane rattled with the assault. Must have been loose in the frame. I reached across and whacked the knocker again two more times. I didn't really expect someone to shoot at me through the door or the glass, but this wasn't a time to take chances.

I heard a faint rattle as an inside door was opened. Then the big outside door beside me cracked a few inches. It was on a chain to keep it from opening wide enough to allow riff raff like me to gain access.

"Afternoon, sir. Can I help you?" Her voice bespoke magnolias and summer breezes and southern Georgia plantations—a place I'd never been.

"I'd like to talk with Mr. George Polk. I believe this is his residence?"

"I'm very sorry, sir, Judge Polk is a mite indisposed this afternoon. If you will give me your card and an indication of why you wish to see him, I'm sure the Judge will be happy to have you make an appointment."

I couldn't see much of my friend on the inside of the door. It was dark behind her. Just a big brown eye part of a nose, and a chunk of mocha-colored skin. I was willing to bet she'd recently come from a much warmer region of our country. I was also pretty sure she made the same speech to everyone who showed up unannounced at the Judge's door. I was also willing to bet a few gold shekels (did they come in gold?) that if I gave the woman my card I'd never get through the door. And since I already knew the Judge almost never left his grand if deteriorating mansion, giving her my card was tantamount to defeat in this quarter.

"Look, ma'am," I whined, "I've come all this way just to see the Judge for a few minutes. I don't have a card, as such, but if you can give me a piece of paper, I can just write him a little note. Do you think that would be all right?"

There was no sense trying to get by this woman with threats. I could see that. I didn't want to threaten her, although I was getting a feeling that threatening the Judge might be in my future. I was also pretty sure I needed to know the whereabouts of a thug I had encountered a few days earlier. One Harlan Ford.

16

The door shut and the woman went away. I stood there, restlessly looking up and down the block. I never really worried about somebody looking for me while I was driving about the city. I pretty much knew every alley byway and boulevard in the Twins. True, South St. Paul wasn't my regular beat, but I grew up a careful and alert driver, thanks to the drivers ed guy in school. Being a P.I. meant never being tailed anywhere. I get in my car and my radar kicks in. So I knew nobody had followed me here to this address. But now I'd been stationary for all of twenty minutes.

The door cracked open again and a slender brown hand snaked out holding a pad of plain white paper and a ball point pen. I looked at them while I thanked the woman and took possession. No advertising on either the cheap white pad of paper or the pen. Totally anonymous.

I scribbled at one corner of the sheet, muttered to myself, changed my mind, tore off the page and stuffed it in my pocket. Then I block printed a note to the Judge telling him I wanted to talk about South St. Paul, a robbery, a Raymond Polk, and the deaths of Kristi and Kent Kava.

I handed the pad and pen back through the still-chained door to my unseen go-between. She shut the door and, presumably, disappeared into the depths of the house. Then I waited. There was really no reason why this gentleman should see me. Other than curiosity. If the judge was involved in any way, his wisest course was to stay far away from me.

I was counting on his ego. In my experience, crooked folk, especially politicians, usually think they're smarter than anyone, particularly if they've been getting away with things for a while. I was becoming persuaded that Judge Polk was in that category. If so, he'd want to know what I knew and maybe try to give me a false lead or two. The common variation was to warn me of dire consequences if I pursued my quest. Either way I'd have a clue as to his thinking and his possible plans. The trick in these kinds of confrontations is to appear dumber than one actually is. Or at least to seem so ignorant of the real facts of the matter as to be easily dismissible.

Well, we'd see, if I even got inside this massive door.

Not a single vehicle had gone by on the quiet street. I listened to the birds in the nearby trees and wished I was off at a lakeside cabin with my sweetie.

The chain rattled and the door swung wide. I had breached the sanctuary!

The woman who now escorted me across a wide expanse of creaking floor, polished, I noted, to a high waxed gloss, was tall, slender but solid, brown in a dark, severely cut dress of modest skirt length that just missed being a maid or housekeeper's uniform. We walked up a broad, gently curving staircase that went around to the right, past tall windows. This was some kind of foyer. Unfortunately one had to be a lot taller than I to see just what sort of view the windows gave. What I saw was a pretty spectacular view of the billowing clouds of white and light gray that moved majestically across the sky from the west.

On the second floor, the house was also wide open, with two long corridors issuing toward the west and east wings of the house, respectively. Behind me now was a balcony railing of polished wood. Directly ahead was a pair of paneled white-painted doors that gave onto a room, I presumed, that rested directly over the front door. It was to these doors that my escort led me. She rapped sharply twice and opened the right-hand door. She half turned and beckoned me to follow her through and we were in the presence of the man himself.

The problem was, of course, that while I knew his name, we had never met and I had not had an opportunity to observe him in the courtroom. I didn't have a clue as to the right protocol. His protocol. Sometimes with these folks, the correct attitude can go a long way toward getting what one wants. I decided aggressive hardball would be wrong at this point. I didn't bow and scrape physically. But I managed a pretty good attitude of deference.

"Judge Polk. Good afternoon, sir. Thank you for seeing me today. I'll try not to take up too much of your time." I took two steps forward toward him where he stood behind his desk.

"Louise?" His voice was low and sandy, as if he'd been too long in the desert on a horse with no name."

She indicated the note I had sent in. Then she turned and walked away. I heard the door snick softly shut. Nobody offered me a seat but I went for one anyway. The overstuffed wing chair about six feet to one side of the desk looked quite comfortable. So I sat and surveyed my adversary, because I was under no illusions that we were just going to have an inconsequential afternoon chat, and neither, I was sure, was the judge.

I glanced around the room while I waited for him to ask the usual question. Behind him and his big wooden desk was a large window that would give a great view of the river and the valley down toward Grey Cloud Island, I was sure, if the heavy drape was opened. On both side walls were built-in bookshelves, mostly filled and I recognized the spines of a set of Westlaw volumes, along with a lot of dark leather-bound tomes that gave substance and gravitas to the room. I wondered how many secrets might be revealed if one had the opportunity to go through the collection. When my gaze came back to him, he was watching me.

"I have a first edition of the opinions of Justice Holmes," he said quietly.

"Oliver Wendell," I smiled. "No thanks, I believe I have the paperback edition at home."

"So, Mr. Sean how can I help you."

I swung my feet back and forth once, then I said, "Judge Polk, your name came up during an investigation I'm doing."

"An investigation? Why is a private citizen interested in me or my family?"

Aha, I thought. Right away he's pointing out that as a PI, I have limited powers. "Well, sir, a member of your family engaged my services to do a background check on an old weapon that was unearthed in their back yard."

"How am I involved?"

"Your grandniece is Kristi Polk Kava. Her son actually found the weapon and the father asked for my help."

"Yes. I am quite sure it was not my grandniece who initiated that request. We are a family given to rectitude and inclined to privacy. She would not have made such a request on her own initiative."

"I wonder, sir. I hate to be the messenger, but are you aware of her death?"

The judge looked down at his desk and his pudgy fingers which lay almost lifeless on the desk top. Except for an occasional twitch. Oppressive silence rushed in and leaned heavily upon us. I listened but even the house seemed to be holding itself tight.

"I shall ask you not to speak of this again, sir," he said in an even lower voice. "Now, please state your business."

"Judge, your grandniece's husband was murdered at the same time and those murders have something to do with a stash of money and a revolver found buried in the back yard of the Kava place a few days ago."

There was no movement from my target. Finally, "I have no information about that so-called discovery."

"Wasn't your father on the bench in Ramsey County when the Railway Express was robbed in South St. Paul back in the early 'thirties?"

"I believe so. That robbery occurred when I was a small child."

I knew that of course, and those facts could be easily checked. But I was fishing for reactions. "How did your father feel about the O'Connor system?" O'Connor was the legendary chief of the St. Paul Police Department who declared the city a safe haven for thieves and robbers and others of that ilk so long as they didn't commit any crimes in the city. It had happened in the late 'twenties and they somehow forgot to include Minneapolis which led to more crime across the river and more passive corruption in the saintly city. The South St. Paul robbery and murder may have had links to some of the thugs who came to Minnesota to enjoy a vacation. But it wasn't those people I was interested in. I was more interested in the links to local folks, such as the Polk families.

"There are voluminous records of my family's struggle against corruption and our long-standing efforts to make this region a better, more law-abiding place, safe to raise families." He said this in the same monotone I'd been subjected to since I entered the room. Oops. I'd opened the door to the Polk family official pronouncements and their struggle to avoid being sullied by accusations of corruption and payoffs. My library research had told of periodic troubles, but while there had been maybe a dozen or so charges made public over the years, Judge Polk—the one on the bench in the 'twenties—had never even been formally charged with anything. Nor had the judge squatting across the desk from me. He hadn't risen as high as his father, but then, the family already had plenty of money and political influence by the time he ascended to his first judicial throne.

"Judge Polk, I wanted to inform you that the revolver I mentioned, remember, the one dug up on the Kava property, has been turned over to the Bureau of Criminal Apprehension for examination and analysis." Right. They'd probably chucked it into a handy dumpster already, but the judge wouldn't know that. Yet. I had no idea how far his tentacles might still reach. I got a reaction. Not much of one, but a flinch, like an annoying horsefly had dive-bombed his nose.

"You indicated you have other questions."

"Yes, Judge. What can you tell me about a Robert Polk who lives over on Ramsey Hill and apparently works for the U.S. post office?"

His mouth twitched in what might have been a smile. "What is your concern with this gentleman?"

"He's a Polk. I'm doing a bit of research among all your relatives," I said.

"The man in question has no connection to the affair you are looking into. Other than his name, he has no known connection to my family and he certainly wasn't alive when the robbery took place. There has been an occasional inquiry in the past about this Robert Polk, so we are familiar with the confusion that can occur.

"Now, young man, was there anything else? Or are you through fishing? I used to throw young detectives who sought warrants for such fishing out of my court. Now it's time for you to leave."

Yes, it was. I'd delivered my message. The revolver was being examined. That was it, and my opportunity to face this man, this fading influential old man. My instinct told me he was unhappy about the finding of that revolver and that the old train robbery was in his awareness. Why would that be unless he knew something more about that seventy-year old crime? Or was it that he was still obsessing after all these years about the robbery as a blot on the family escutcheon.

So I said goodbye, turned as the door opened and my guide smiled and beckoned me. She led me back down the wide gently curving staircase. The walls were bare. No august self-important nineteenth or twentieth century portraits. No art. In fact, although I hadn't seen the entire house, there didn't seem to be art of any kind. No rural scenes by American or French painters. No small statuary of nymphs or satyrs, or birds, for that matter. Maybe he'd been selling it off. I didn't notice any places on the walls where frames might have hung in the recent past. I started to wonder about his financial health, something I hadn't paid any attention to up to now, but I was going to have to do some more research into the life and times of this judge and his family.

Yes indeedy.

17

From my office I called Sam Monroe, the South St. Paul detective responsible for investigating the shooting of his colleague, Detective McKinley. He had nothing to tell me, except that they hadn't made a decision as to who would take over the dead officer's duties. I wondered about the cold case file. Monroe said he thought it wasn't a high priority.

"I can't help thinking that something in McKinley's activity with your cold cases might be the motive."

"Well, you'll have to discuss that with the Chief," Monroe said as he rang off.

Right. I had about as much chance of persuading the Chief of the South St. Paul PD to follow my suggestions as Satan had climbing a ladder to get back into heaven. Monroe apparently considered me at least partially responsible for the death of Tom McKinley, and I wasn't sure he wasn't partially right. I couldn't shake the feeling that the bullet that killed the detective was meant for me.

Nor did the police in White Bear Lake have anything to say to me other than Hello and no and goodbye. Things were really moving forward. Why, I was afraid I'd be running full tilt down the street before long, just to keep up with these rapid developments. The problem was, as we all know, that the longer it takes to make any significant headway in these cases, the longer they tend to drag on and the harder they are to bring to a satisfactory conclusion. Then the telephone rang. It was my BCA friend Ann Hoover.

"Just what are you playing at, Sean?"

"Excuse me?"

Long, heartfelt sigh. "Phone calls, Sean, questions. People stopping me on the way to lunch with more questions."

"Lunch? Like that barbecue place we went to over on East Seventh?"

"Don't try to change the subject. The team leader in the weapons section is grumbling he can't get his work done because of all the questions about that revolver you brought in. Reporters, for God's sake!"

I smiled with satisfaction. The gossip mill was healthy. Stanley Jackson had been talking. And I bet the judge had added to the volume. "But of course, nobody from the BCA is saying anything because it's an open case, right?"

"It is now. Turns out there's some DNA evidence under all that rust. DNA that is most likely not from underground critters."

My interest rose and I sat up in my chair. "You found some DNA to analyze? Phenomenal. I always knew you were a genius. What do you have?"

"Don't get your knickers in a twist," Ann said. "You know it takes a minimum of seventy-two hours, even in a high profile rush situation."

"Yes but—"

"And I'm not the one doing the testing."

"You aren't?"

"No, fool. Personal connection with you. There are ethical considerations so I turned it over to another scientist. You had to know that would happen."

I nodded at the telephone. "Sure, Ann, I guess I did at that. So when do you think you'll have a result?"

"Week, maybe. But it could be sooner if the sample is too degraded to be of any use."

"Why faster in that case?

"Because we wouldn't run a full set of tests. We've talked about these factors before. These tests take time and the rule is no opinions until all tests ordered are complete and analyzed."

"Yeah, O.K. I guess I expected this. It's just frustrating, this case, I mean."

"What do your training manuals say? Who's that writer? I remember, Jon Jackson."

"Fang Mulheisen?" I thought a minute, couldn't remember anything relevant. Then I laughed. "I've apparently been talking to you too much, telling you about my secret research books. Later." I chuckled some more and hung up the telephone.

I decided on an early night. I almost always take the stuff out of my pockets before I hang up my pants. Pile change and stuff on my bureau. The partial note to the judge that I'd started earlier that day had gone missing. No big deal, one less piece of paper to toss in the trash.

That evening, the call came at precisely eleven-fifteen, and a few seconds. I'm not in the habit of answering late-night calls. They almost always mean trouble. Must be some kind of cosmic rule, or something. In this instance, I was hoping for a call from Catherine. She was in Rochester, I thought, talking to hospital administrators about therapy contract possibilities.

The voice in my ear was a low throaty rasp that conjured up long nights laced with a thick atmosphere of cigarettes and bad booze. The man on the phone when I picked up, didn't waste time with normal communication like identification, or even a casual Hello.

"Hyatt," he said and the phone went dead.

What a cliché, I thought. I'd recognized the voice. It was distinctive and it was a voice I'd heard in radio and TV interviews about important trials and verdicts. And I knew more about him from feature stories in the Sunday newspapers. He was a VIP. We had a long history of occasional connections, although we'd never met. I'd never seen him in action in court, but I understood he was a tough opponent. The guy was a very prominent Minneapolis attorney. Why did he want to talk to me and why in the middle of the night?

I got dressed and drove to the downtown Hyatt. There he was in the bar, sitting alone at a table against one wall. I watched from the door for a moment. When he leaned forward and took the tumbler in his gnarled fist he showed all the authority of a man who'd spent years making the identical gesture in bars and saloons all over the world. He didn't raise his eyes when I sauntered forward. He was sitting alone, but I knew his keeper would be close by.

He took a drink, the heavy shoulder muscles rippling smoothly under the garish short sleeved shirt, some sort of loud flowered print, he wore. Winter and summer, he wore a light-weight short sleeved shirt. Usually with heavy colors and in a bold print. I thought it was meant to show off his physique, which it certainly did.

His name was George Van Buren. Attorney at Law. His heavy head was adorned with thick almost completely gray hair, cropped short on top with no part. Below his bulbous veined nose Van Buren sported a thick moustache styled to bend straight down on either side of his mouth and hung a couple of inches below his chin. A seriously drooping handlebar. He and Kinky Friedman could start a brother act. I made a quick visual sweep of the room and spotted his wife. I'd never met her, either, but she too was recognizable, being never very far from his side, so I'd seen pictures of her. A tall straight-backed woman with a luxurious fall of shiny black hair alleviated by two startlingly white streaks, one over each ear. She had a glass in front of her filled with what was probably club soda and ice. Somewhere I'd heard that she never drank alcohol. Her quick glance registered my presence when I sauntered forward.

I pulled out a chair and sat down across from the man.

The hand he wrapped around the highball glass was scarred and the knuckles were swollen with arthritis. An angry-looking scar ran up the back of his hand across the wrist, almost to his elbow. From a knife wielded by a client who didn't get the result in court he thought he should have, or so the story went.

I nodded at Van Buren and waved the waiter away.

"Have a drink. On me." His voice was low and rumbling, as if it took supreme effort to get the words out.

I raised my eyebrows. Van Buren had a reputation for never buying drinks for anybody, including himself if he could manage it. "No thanks. What can I do for you?"

"I owe you some thanks."

I waited. He breathed. Heavily. He took another drink which almost depleted the liquid in his glass. It was not a small highball glass.

A waitress appeared with a full tumbler of the amber fluid in which floated a single ice cube. She gave me a glass of water.

"My grandniece sends thanks. If her daughter was old enough to know what had happened, she'd thank you too. Maria Van Buren."

Ah, that explained it. The toddler I'd found in the old smoke house near Langton Lake. Not so surprising. Van Buren had a large home not many blocks north of my own. Must have been why his grand niece was lost on my path, not that I owned it or anything. I suppose my taxes supported it though. Hell of an elaborate way to manufacture an excuse for a meeting.

I waited. Van Buren sighed and finished what was obviously not his first drink. "I understand you are looking into an old case."

"I am?"

He fixed me with a beady look. At least I thought so. His eyes were so sunken I couldn't be sure what he was looking at in the dim light of the bar. "I am," I said again, with all the innocence of a newborn babe.

"I am in a position to be of some assistance in the matter at hand."

He talked like a lawyer. "In what way?"

"Don't be arrogant, young man. I have connections throughout the community. You know that." Van Buren stopped and gasped for air. I was alarmed, but when I eyeballed his spouse, she seemed unperturbed. "I am perhaps more familiar with the case than even you, although with your reputation, I expect you already have quite a bit of information, which, one day, you may be willing to share."

Share? What the Hell was going on here? George Van Buren, attorney at law, was one of those strange Midwestern characters that turn up periodically. From where no one is ever sure. One especially doesn't look too closely at the source of their capital. They make an unremarked and unremarkable entrance into a city—Minneapolis, or Chicago, for example. Or maybe Omaha. Over time they exert effort and become influential and pretty soon everyone knows who they are, or at least they think they do. Waiters and especially headwaiters recognize them and defer to them. These are the shadowy characters who populate the avenues and boulevards of fly-over land, the bland, vanilla land, so called, of the Midwest. It was rife with exotic characters like Van Buren who tended to be involved in bizarre happenings, like this incident with his grandniece. Like some of the people who inhabit our State Fair every year.

So I knew Van Buren, or at least I knew about him. What was fact or fiction was difficult to sort out. There'd been no reason for me to even wonder about that. Before. But now we were involved, sort of, because his grand-niece happened to send her daughter off to an athletic field where she lost track at a time when I happened to be waltzing around a lake. Coincidence, some would say. Mere happenstance. It'd never work in a good detective novel.

But I knew that coincidence, the chance intersection of two

lives, can and often is what weaves together a fabric that frequently has significant influence over our actions. So I paid attention. "Mr. Van Buren, are you perhaps acquainted with a South St. Paul judge named Polk?"

Van Buren thought. At least I assumed that's what he was doing during a pause that stretched for at least half a minute, or more. He wasn't drinking, and he wasn't moving. I was pretty sure he was breathing. Finally, just when I was starting to seriously consider becoming alarmed, he shifted his not inconsiderable weight to one haunch. Then he ponderously raised one hand from where it was positioned grasping his highball, and scratched his prominent nose.

"As it happens, I am," he growled. "I have appeared before that magistrate from time to time."

"There was a train robbery in the 'thirties. I think the judge was involved."

"He's not that old," huffed Van Buren. "At that time he'd have been a mere child."

"True, but his father was on the bench at the time, his family values its long-standing prominence in the community and some strange things are happening in this decade which lead me to wonder if he, the current living Judge Polk, retired though he may be, isn't involved, perhaps in a cover-up."

Van Buren raised his head to look at me. This action required him to reposition his trunk, his shoulders and then his head. It took a minute or two and I wondered if he had a seriously bad back, maybe a fused vertebrae or two. I thought perhaps his time as a roustabout in the wildcat days of the Texas and Oklahoma oil fields, if that was even true, might have returned to exact its revenge for helping to deplete from Mother Earth all that fossil fuel. I said none of those things.

Then he smiled, I guess. It was not a pretty sight; he was not wearing all his front teeth. He must have owned a plate he wore in court or for photographs. "I have no way of knowing about that. I understand you have a pistol?"

I nodded. Van Buren wasn't talking about my personal arsenal.

"Guns. Dangerous weapons have been known to reveal interesting facts." He subsided and I realized Van Buren had just told me what this late night meeting was about. He'd never admit it, under oath or in casual conversation, but he had confirmed that one of my working hypothesizes was on target, aimed at the bulls eye. Not something you'd expect a defense lawyer to do, unless something else was going on, something he didn't like one little bit.

Van Buren has just confirmed for me that the rusty revolver I'd found was an important piece of evidence. I'd already decided that, but it was nice to have my thinking confirmed by an outside source. I nodded, saluted him with my glass of water and left the bar without a backward glance.

18

"So, you met the g.m."

I smiled at my lady who was standing in her walk-in closet disrobing, an act I always observed with great pleasure. "General Motors? General Manager? I don't think so."

"You know who I mean. The Great Man, George Van Buren, Attorney at Law. Do you know he's an investor in my company?"

I sat up in bed. "He is? The Great Man invests in massage therapy schools? How big an investor?"

"Relax. Not major and it's through one of his investment companies. Only a few hundred shares. I'll be surprised if he even knows the connection."

"Huh, I'll be surprised if he doesn't," I said. I never liked it when I found connections between my love's life and my detective life. Because of her successful and growing massage school and significant number of important local contracts, plus her canny investment counselors, I encountered traces of her money management from time to time, meaning investors, attorneys, brokers, like that. Those were the troubled upper shelf folks I dealt with in my business. The other folks I dealt with, those on all the lower shelves of our society, those more on my level, didn't know Catherine, or her businesses. But I was learning to live with it. And to be honest I liked the perks her money brought us.

Being your typical lone-wolf-out-of-the-mainstream cliché of a private detective didn't mean I couldn't and didn't appreciate the finer comforts and pleasures of life. The fact that after I stalked the mean streets of the sleeping city, packing iron, dueling with resident evil, I could often go on home to this finely furnished pad, a lovely loving woman and a really good dinner complete with crystal, linen and silver was not lost on me. Mike Hammer, rest his soul, I was not. No cheap walk-up pad for this boy.

"Have you met the mysterious GM?" I said, welcoming my love to bed.

"Nope. Only one or two of his cadre of investment folks.

"Van Buren had his grandniece stashed in that old smoke house so I'd find her and he'd have an excuse to contact me."

"What?" Catherine sat up in bed. "That's appalling."

"Yeah, I think so too, but now I'm pretty sure there was more to it than I saw at the time. I'd bet a large sum of money, if I had it, that the girl was constantly under guard, I just didn't realize it."

"I still say that's disgusting."

"Van Buren has a rep for being paranoid. He's known for meeting people outside his office. The meetings are often set up at the last minute. He seems to think he's under constant surveillance, wiretaps, cameras and so on."

"What a way to live. Was the meeting worth it?"

"Umm. I think so. I'll check of course, but I'll bet another large sum of money I don't have that his firm represents Harlan Ford."

"No kidding!"

I smiled sleepily, kissed her bare hip and closed my eyes as I rolled over. Being a P.I. can be exhausting.

* * * *

The next morning I located Detective First Class Stanley Jackson at his office in White Bear. He confirmed that the law firm that had represented Mr. Ford was a prominent Minneapolis criminal defense business, Cerf and Van Buren. What a surprise! Nobody I knew had seen or personally talked to Cerf in years. I had no idea what his first name might be. Maybe there was no Cerf. It was an interesting connection that Van Buren was representing the felon I'd apprehended in Kava's yard. Then he'd used his infant niece in an elaborate ploy to get me to meet him at a bar in downtown Minneapolis. Apparently that was to give me a message that I was going in the right direction by concentrating on the revolver. Not normal behavior for a defense attorney in the service of his client. Observers might just figure our brief meeting at the Hyatt was only his way of thanking me for rescuing his grandniece.

I was already focused on the revolver, but Van Buren had had no way of knowing that. So he had reached out to set me on the righteous path. Van Buren wasn't acting like a normal defense attorney. I had no information how Van Buren really felt about his family, but there were always ways to reach out to someone. The telephone, for instance. He'd had no right and no need to possibly endanger that little girl. On the other hand, his paranoia may have been in overdrive. I'd have to talk to the cops. Maybe they could charge him with reckless endangerment or something. Meanwhile, I had a judge and a killer to run down. There was also a Ford in my future.

I called my friend Jerry Ford, a prosecutor in Ramsey County. "Jer, I need a small favor. It concerns one of your ex-judges, George Polk, and a practicing attorney, George Van Buren." I stopped for a reaction. Jerry was silent. "Huh," I went on. "Two Georges. That's a little confusing. And I seem to have two Fords here. More confusion. Could he be a relative of yours?"

"What are you going on about?" Impatience in Jerry's voice.

"It's just that I prefer cases in which everybody has a different name. Less confusing that way."

A sigh. "What is it you want to know, exactly?"

"Connections. Between the Georges. George One and George Two. Tenuous, possibly. Intimate, perhaps. Frankly, I'm looking for some little thread I can use to unravel the Kava murder thing out in White Bear Lake. Or maybe weave a net and catch a big tuna. Can you help?"

"Not too difficult. I'll run searches on the databases. The information is all in the public record. You could try the library. Which George is One and which is Two?"

I chuckled. "Haven't figured that out yet. But you'll be happy to know this minor thug going by the name of Harlan Ford appears to be involved as well."

"Not one of my relatives," he grunted.

We parted company, still friends. I knew that Jerry was going to do more than just search a public database. Then I called Ricardo Simon with a similar request. I didn't have any tight contact in Washington County or in any of the other counties that make up what we call the metropolitan area. So I was going to start with our central cities and see where that led, if anywhere. I was in need of my next-door friends at my office. Belinda and Betsy Revulon, who did amazing things with computers could design searches that would crawl into tiny fissures in the web of technology that entangled us all and find links I could later follow on my own and tease into giving up what I needed to know. Sadly, they were not available so I was forced to rely on my own devices.

I drove to the city hall of South St. Paul. There I presented myself to the city clerk's office and was directed to a clean well-lighted place where old public court records were stored. I discovered the city staff maintained a well-kept index that told me several things of more than passing interest.

George Polk and George Van Buren had indeed crossed swords. Several times, in fact, they had seen each other in court, one on the bench the other defending various miscreants. So far so good.

I made a few notes and went looking for a Polk who was not named George. George Polk's legendary father had apparently not done business as a judge or even as a young attorney, if the city's records were to be believed. I went off to Hastings, seat of Dakota County, wherein I was able to determine that Attorney Polk, later Judge Polk, had had an office for a long time in the 'twenties and 'thirties of the previous century in the brawling livestock processing city of South St. Paul. His cases often involved stockyard workers who, apparently not satisfied with the hard physical labor of their jobs butchering and processing cattle, hogs and sheep, occasionally fell to fighting at one or more of the many bars and public houses that lined the streets of the commercial district of the city.

I showed the address to one of the young workers and she said, "I'll get you the locator." She then disappeared into a far back room.

"Here," she said a few minutes later. "This works sort of like a telephone book. Beside each address is a code that will locate the address on the map here." She handed me a tattered book with a handwritten label on the grimy cover that said "1918 to 1938."

I quickly found the address of the law offices of Charles Polk, Esq. I realized that the street was the same street on which the train robbers had turned when making their retreat from the siding which held the Railway Express car.

I went off the library of the Minnesota Historical Society where I was able, with the help 'of a pleasant and efficient librarian, to find some pictures of the street where it all started. And lo, there in one fine print from what the photographers call a large-format negative, was a crisp black and white image of a building and also there, plain as day, on the window of that office building only a block from the police station, in lovely bold script, was the legend Charles Polk: Attorney at Law. I was willing to bet that had senior Polk been standing in his window that fateful noon, he would have seen, no doubt with horror filled eyes, a cousin or maybe a nephew, anyway a relative of his, standing in the back of a fast moving truck, gun down the hapless rookie policeman, Eddie Washington. Coincidence? Nah, not on your tintype.

The records of the inquiry, the police investigation at the time, never mentioned an eyewitness account of either the actual robbery or the high-speed, well, high speed for that era, getaway that resulted in the murder of the patrol officer. That would have been the time for an upstanding member of the bar to reluctantly come forward and point a finger at his relative. But it hadn't happened.

Did young Polk, after killing the officer, chance to look up and fix his panicky gaze on his older relative, standing, stunned, in the window of that law office? Also interesting to me was what might have devolved over the years from Charles Polk's sin of omission. Overly dramatic? Perhaps. I knew the answers to those questions were probably lost forever. I also knew it would take the kind of persistent research I wasn't ever going to do to find, in some dusty archives, what might have resulted from that chance connection. But I was damn sure the murders of the Kavas were connected to these Polks.

I looked further but didn't find any other pictures in the Historical Society files that were helpful, so I paid for a digital copy of the one and left the building.

19

My destination was the South St. Paul City Hall and police department. When I arrived and swung in to a visitor's parking spot, I spied detective Monroe walking hurriedly toward a car idling at the curb.

"Detective," I called.

Monroe waved me off. "Go see the Chief," he called back as he slid into the white late-model Chevy and he and the driver, whom I couldn't identify, roared off. So much for getting together over tea and scones. Still, I hadn't called ahead, had I?

I wasn't ready to visit with the chief of police, but on reflection, decided it wouldn't hurt and might advance my understanding of the case. I went upstairs. The chief, according to his receptionist, was indeed in and available if I'd care to wait a few minutes. I gave her a business card, smiled and sat in a hard chair against one wall of the smallish reception area.

After a few minute, a portly uniformed gentleman exited the chief's office and with a nod in my general direction, disappeared into the hallway. The young and pert receptionist smiled brightly, answered a page from her telephone and said to me, "You may go in now, Mr. Sean."

No hesitation in her voice. I liked that. Inside a somewhat larger, sun-filled, essentially square office, Chief of Police Andre Johnson stood up behind his double pedestal desk watching me cross his carpet to within hand-shaking distance. We shook in a civilized manner and I sat where he gestured. I gazed up at his. He was tall and slender and appeared to be in good shape, the very model of a modern cop.

"You certainly got here promptly."

"Excuse me?" I adjusted the knees of my pant legs even though there was no crease to worry about. I looked up at him. "Did you summon me?"

"I did. Barely two hours ago. When one of my officers is murdered I take a close personal interest in the case." He nodded as if he felt he'd said something in just the right way.

"You know of my presence at the shooting of Detective McKinley two days ago."

"Of course."

"Even though I didn't know you were reaching out to me, I'm here because I wanted to tell you up front how sorry I am. Is there a fund for Detective McKinley?"

"No sir, not yet. There will be and I'll be happy to inform you when the details are arranged."

"I assume you also know how I happen to be involved?"

The chief leaned forward and frowned. "Yeah, I sure do. Which is why I wanted to talk with you." His veneer of politeness was dissipating like a scudding cloud in a stiff breeze.

"There's not much more I can say at this time. You've read the reports from the scene. I don't know much of anything more now, except I want to help in any way I can to nab the guy who did this."

"Uh huh. You're a private citizen. I don't care about your P.I. license." His voice was going perilously close to a sneer. "I want everything you know about this event and I want it soonest."

"Chief, you're entitled to your opinion about private investigators, but I have some background in this case and I think collaboration, or at least cooperation is a good idea. I want to show you a photograph and ask you what you think." Without waiting for a response, I slid the 8x10 glossy photograph out of the envelope and across his desk. Diverted from his agenda, he picked up the picture, as I hoped he would.

"What am I looking at?"

"It's a street scene that's pretty close to what the skells saw in 'thirty-three after they took down the Express car and drove away. When they drove out of town and shot Patrolman Eddie Washington."

Chief Johnson stared at me for a moment. Then he looked at the photograph. Then he looked back at me. "So?"

"Look closely. You've seen the photos on the robbery that are in your files. I know you have. This one isn't from that file."

Intrigued, probably in spite of himself, he looked more closely. "This was taken a long time after. Years probably."

"Correct. But the buildings haven't changed. Have they."

"Where'd you get this?"

"Minnesota Historical Society. Apparently somebody who was interested in the unsolved murder and robbery made some pictures. The file notes say it was maybe two years after the actual event."

"What's your point?" The chief still held the photograph in both hands.

"Look closely. Maybe you want a magnifying glass?"

He peered at the photograph again. Watching his face, I could see when he found it.

"Son of a bitch!" he exclaimed. "I'll be damned. There it is, right on the window. Polk and Gardner, Attorneys at Law." Then the chief made the same connection I had.

"He coulda been standin' right there in the window, watchin'. Hell he coulda been waiting to see it go down."

"Who are we talking about here? Who could have been watching?"

"You know damn well who! Judge Mr. High and Mighty

Moral Polk, that's who!" Then he reconsidered after a sharp look at me.

In spite of the buzz I was getting in my gut, I kept a bland sort of mildly inquiring expression on my face. Looking stupid has never steered me wrong.

"Wait a minute. This can't be right. No," Johnson said, figuring the years in his head, "It's the office of the old man, Judge Polk's father."

"Right," I said. "And we have no way of knowing if he was in that window when it all happened, or maybe he'd deliberately arranged to be out of town, even."

Sparks of conspiracy zinged in the chief's eyes as he leaned over the picture toward me. I could sense it happening. "You know, Sean, you're not just some dumbass private dick. You could be on to something here."

I ignored his backhanded crack and laid out my current theory, the one this dumbass investigator had come up with all on his own.

"A question has occurred to me," I said as I wound up my summary." You had an interesting reaction to the picture. Care to explain?"

Chief Johnson stared at me for a moment. "No. I don't think so. And you'll be wise to forget you heard it."

I figured he wasn't ready to trust me all the way yet. But then he said, "I'm gonna give Monroe a heads up it's okay for the two of you to stay in touch until we get this moke who murdered Tom."

"As I suggested, I think the murders of the Kavas and the killing of your detective are part of the same deal. Somebody has unleashed a killer dog. What we need is a motive."

"When will the BCA release their findings? Do you have anything on that?"

I hesitated for a millisecond. It wasn't that I didn't trust the chief, I just didn't trust him enough. "Can't say, sir. While we wait for whatever that revolver will give us, it would help, I think, if we can get a handle on the present Judge Polk and his career."

Johnson looked at me over the desk with a shrewd gaze. He was no fool, and I could almost see his shifting stance on how far he wanted to let me in on this case. "I've known the judge since he started his practice, right there in that office." His big forefinger tapped the photograph for emphasis. "We've got a database. I can get a list of court appearances he made as an attorney and after he became a judge."

I raised one eyebrow. It's something I practice. You can say a lot with an eyebrow twitch. And the best part is nobody really knows for absolute fact what you mean with it. So I can change my mind if things don't work out. "That might be very informative."

"It's only what he's done here in the city. Well, I guess there are a few cases from outside. We like to keep tabs on our judges." He smiled mirthlessly.

I stood. "Chief Johnson. I appreciate the confidence." I stuck out a hand. My right one. Hell, I've got a little class. "We're gonna nail this sucka, whoever he might be. I'll be in touch."

He frowned, the chief did, and touched my hand with his fingers in a kind of phantom shake. I wheeled and strode to the door, trying to project a jauntiness, a confidence I didn't entirely feel. He let me get the door open before he growled at me, "Don't fuck this up, Sean."

I waved a hand as I went out. Hot and cold this chief blew, hot and cold, like the prairie winds in North Dakota.

20

I drove to my office. The light on my message machine was blinking. My silent partner who never slept, never took a day off and never complained had taken a message for me. I punched the buttons and listened. I liked the voice—it was Catherine, but I didn't care for the message one bit.

"I don't want to worry you, honey, but I think you should know about this." The recording didn't do justice to the quality of her voice, but her concern came through, loud and clear. "I've been getting some strange calls on the unlisted number. They started last night. Now I've had two today, threatening messages on the recorder. I also had a call at work, that one was just heavy breathing and then a hang-up."

I mashed the auto-dial button and reached the phone in Catherine's apartment. To my immense relief, she picked up on the third ring.

"Hey, sweetheart."

"Oh, Sean. When you get here, stop at the desk and pick up a package, please. UPS just delivered it."

"I got your message. Any more crap?"

"No, but now I'm thinking I might be overreacting."

"Maybe, but we aren't taking any chances. I'll be there as soon as possible. It bothers me that whoever it is has your unlisted number. I'm gonna look into that too."

I closed the office and went down to the lot behind the building where my car was parked. An observer might have thought I was so focused on those calls—had they known about them—the caller, for instance, that I was unaware of my surroundings. That observer would have been wrong. I didn't get to be almost 40, with a lot of years as an investigator, because I'm stupid or prone to taking chances. If I walk or run into a situation, I'm up, I'm ready. I'm like Bill Smith. You won't find me waltzing into a strange cemetery at two in the ayem chasing a stone killer with nothing but my two hands and no backup.

I jumped in my tired Taurus and kicked the bull into action. Nobody followed me into Kenwood, home of my Catherine. I remembered her request and stopped at the office on the main floor. The package was small, brown and ordinary looking. I elevatored to the fourth floor and entered the apartment I share with the lady, my lovely tall wealthy massage therapist. She insists that I don't pay any rent. Of course, she owns the building, under a corporate name or two that conceal her real identity from the actual operators and tenants of the place.

I contribute in other ways, she says. I do, I do. The ways may not be exactly what you're thinking though. "Catherine," I called, closing the door to the hall. I tugged the knob to be sure the latch was secure.

"In here, toots. I'm getting some help from the cable folks tracing these annoying calls."

I dropped the package on the hall table and sauntered down to the smallest of the three bedrooms, the one that acted as her office and exercise room. She was sitting at her computer fingers racing over the keys as she responded to questions from someone at her communication company. She had a bundled service, Internet, television and digital telephone. It made a convenient package and probably saved some money. It also gave us access to good quality communication. I didn't care one way or the other about some of the services, but good reliable telephone and internet service was important to my work. I also like my music with good scotch and good cheese, so it better be listenable.

Not long after it became clear we were a couple for the long haul, I had contributed a serious sound system and wired it through the place. Our TV watching, other than news, wasn't much but we had a DVD player attached to the set in the bedroom where we watched movies from a mostly prone position.

My friend—I never am quite sure what to call her; girlfriend sounds high-schoolish and partner has other connotations. Lover is too personal for the people you encounter on the street, or at the civic and social fundraisers Catherine dragged me to with increasing frequency. SO or significant other sounds pretentious. My friend was sitting at her computer dressed in jeans and a huge baggy U of M gray sweatshirt with the sleeves pushed up above her elbows. The smile she beamed my way seemed to dim the sunlight radiating through the windows behind her. Maybe I'm biased.

I kissed her and she kissed me back. The computer screen showed some kind of chart. Excel maybe? I didn't know. I can call up emails and type and save notes. Other stuff I leave to my friends down the hall, the Revulon cousins. Catherine has offered to help when I get stuck and Betsey or Belinda isn't available. Like now. But I didn't like to do that, get her involved in my cases. Inevitably a private investigator like myself deals with some pretty sordid circumstances. Catherine, raised on a farm in South Dakota, wasn't necessarily exposed to the seamier side of life, especially murder. I didn't see any reason to extend her education in that direction if I could help it.

After a leisurely collaborative dinner, during which Catherine was at pains to assure me that a few odd hang-ups on the telephone were nothing to worry about, we cleaned up in companionable silence, save for the clatter of tableware. She had reminded me again that in her early years getting nasty calls was part of the landscape, and when she first opened her school and won a good contract from a medium-sized but fairly prominent law firm with offices in Edina, some of the wives of partners and associates in the firm mounted a campaign to get the contract cancelled. There were calls at all hours of the night, threatening calls, insulting calls. She was called whore, accused of running an outcall prostitution service, and threatened with all sorts of retribution, stopping just short of murder.

"I learned even earlier when I started in this business that a lot of people just assume masseuses are dressed up prosties." She raised a pretty shoulder and smirked at me. "Fact is, as you know well, more than a few prostitution operations masquerade as massage parlors. Especially outcall networks."

"There are always people ready to think the worst of somebody else. Here's what I'm going to do. I'll get some acquaintances I know to run some traces on your phone. We'll capture incoming numbers. If this doofus calls again, we'll locate him, or they," I amended, "and I'll pay him a little visit. I have to tell you I don't like the timing. There's the possibility that these calls are a way to try to get at me."

"The Kavas?"

"Yeah.

The next morning I reached out to some specialists whose names I had in my little black book. The one I never carry. The one I keep in a place I made behind a concrete block in my Roseville basement. My other domicile where I was spending less and less time. I chiseled out the hole originally, but then I discovered that insects and the damp were slowly working on the paper in my book. So naturally, I called one of the experts in my book. He came and fixed me a nice metal insert that was bug and damp-proof. And nearly detection proof. That had happened several years ago and now someone else from my list of specialists was going to help me with Catherine's hang-up problem.

The specialists I called this time were electronics craftsmen who knew everything there was to know about quietly bugging telephone and cable lines. I explained what I needed, a trace on Catherine's digital phones, at work and at home, that might give me a lead to the caller. I knew it might be a waste of time. The guy might never call again, or the trace might lead to one of those increasingly rare phenomena, a public phone in some bar, or in a parking ramp, or even on a lonely street corner, but I was going to try.

Meanwhile, I needed to check on my boy, Alex Kava. So I called the house. Alex himself answered. "Hey, buddy, this is Sean. Remember me?"

"Sure, Mr. Sean. How's the detective business?"

"It's pretty good. Can I talk to your aunt?"

"Sure, she's right here." I heard him hand off the phone and Susan Polk came on. We exchanged pleasantries and I asked her if she'd had any recent harassing calls or hang-ups.

"No, nothing at all. I do have an answering service, because we sometimes get lots of begging calls. I don't quite understand why that happens when I'm on a no-call list. And then there are the calls during the silly season."

I smiled. "I guess you mean the election season."

"That's exactly it, Mr. Sean. Now that Alex is out of summer school, you know, we're going to the family lake cabin." She dropped her voice. "I thought it would be good for Alex. He loves swimming and fishing. It'll help get dark things out of his head."

"Good idea. How's he doing?"

"Children are remarkably resilient, you know. He has sad moments, more than he should, but he's all right, I think. The doctor and his nurses tell me he's doing quite well."

"It sounds like some time in a cabin up north is a good solution," I said. Not for me; up north conjuring visions of boats, rocky beaches, bugs and sand in all the wrong places. I thought having the boy out of town until this thing was settled was good. We said our goodbyes and I got Alex to promise to write at least once. The kid was growing on me.

My immediate task was to get a line on the guy who tried to dent my skull with a cosh, back there in the Kava rear yard. I called my friend Ricardo Simon. "Lunch?" I asked. "On me."

"Sure, Sean. Lurt's over on south thirty-eighth? Twelve-thirty? Do I have to bring something?"

"Only whatever you can turn up on a felon named Harlan Ford. See you then."

Twelve-thirty came and went. I'd secured a table against one wall where we wouldn't be easily overheard. I hoped there wasn't a major upheaval in the city that had kept detective Simon from making our rendezvous. The TV set over the bar was tuned to a local channel and I didn't see any momentous events being chronicled. Then he was there, slipping in through the back door, past the necessaries and the office.

Lurts was a long-time neighborhood institution that had outgrown its neighborhood and become known pretty much all over the metro area for its juicy beef hamburgers. A tattered sign stapled to the wall behind the long scarred wooden bar proclaimed the attitude of the cook: WELL-DONE BEEF AIN'T. Regardless of the efforts of the Agricultural Department, the FDA and probably the Surgeon General to the contrary, this grill refused to ever deliver any ground beef in a patty that was darker than pink in the center. Carnivores who were worried about food-borne diseases from undercooking were encouraged to look elsewhere for their beef. This recalcitrance on the part of the cook and owner didn't appear to have any negative effect on the level of patronage. The dark place was crowded with late nooners.

"How ya doin'?" Ricardo said, sliding into the chair across from me. "I see you chose a table by itself, instead of one of our booths. This must be serious."

I nodded and got right to it. "This guy, Ford, attacked me. After I suitably subdue and disarm him, the White Bear cops take him away. So far so good, *comprende*?"

"If you say so."

"Then, a day or so later, I discover that he is out on bond, released through the good offices of, to sort of quote the cop, an important associate of a very high-powered attorney in these here twin cities. So now I'm wondering, because said cop won't tell me who the attorney is, what sort of juice this Ford fellow has. And I need to have a face to face with this Ford fellow so I reached out and tapped you. In the hopes this Ford fellow is likely known to you fine folk."

"Do you say that a lot?"

"Say what?"

"Ford fellow."

I just looked at Ricardo silently. He grinned. I grinned back.

"It happens," he continued, "that this Ford fellow has a record. Actually, quite a long record of thuggery of various kinds. Here and in other jurisdictions."

"So, be upstanding and forthcoming, good sir. I desire a local current address."

"I checked with his parole officer."

"My eyebrows went up at that. "He has a parole officer?"

"Yes, he's on parole and should not have been released by the folks in White Bear. There is some discussion going on about lack of cooperation or at least lack of communication between departments as a result of his premature release."

"You don't think there might be a scent of rot in the system?"

Simon shook his head. "Nope, just communications foul-up. Also high-powered connections." He slid a piece of paper across the table. I put down my coffee cup and scanned the paper. A handwritten scribble of an address, a couple of names and phone numbers I didn't recognize—I can't know every thug in town—

and an attorney's number. That I did know. It was the number for an office officially considered to be that of George Van Buren, the eminent criminal attorney. I looked at my friend.

He nodded. "Yeah, our good buddy Van B. He's listed as the attorney of record, although I assume he doesn't act directly, except occasionally in court."

"Something very odd is going on here. How does a low-life like this Ford fellow have the stones to engage the likes of a heavyweight like Van Buren? Even if he has the money in some offshore account you don't know about. Pro bono for Van Buren?"

Simon nodded. "Possibly. More likely a favor for a friend."

A thought occurred to me. "Do you know how long this unusual and nefarious association has existed?"

"My sketchy information says about a week."

"A week? Do you realize it was only last Tuesday that this guy tried to brain me? Curiouser and curiouser." I wondered to myself what V.I. Warshawski would think about such circumstances. Her cases in Chicago seemed to get stranger and more convoluted as time went on, but Paretsky dealt with serious social issues while telling a good story. Follow the money, somebody once said. Trouble was, the only money I had at the moment was a pile of smelly scraps. And even those were no longer in my possession.

21

I decided I ought to visit the judge again, but first I needed to understand what his relationship was with the people I was encountering on the fringes of the train robbery and the more recent murders. Was it possible Judge Polk senior was somehow involved and no one had figured it out even after all these years? Or maybe someone had indeed figured out that the judge's father was dirty and was blackmailing him. People like the judge put a lot of store in the good name of their family. They didn't take kindly to slander and libel. Besmirching the Polk escutcheon with something messy like blackmail would be a dangerous game.

But first things first, I was on my way to the address of record of my good friend, Harlan Ford. He who had tried to brain me with that length of pipe in the Kava back yard a few days ago. Ford lived in a crummy walkup on a short street in south Minneapolis. The houses on the block all seemed to need some maintenance. The one I sought had a broken screen door, a head-high chain link fence that effectively isolated the front yard from the street, and an open front stoop that hadn't seen a paintbrush in this century.

I parked in one of the numerous empty spaces I found along the curbs on both sides of the street. Either these folks drove to work or, more likely, they used public transportation and didn't own automobiles.

I deliberately parked down the block three doors from my target address. If Ford was in, I wanted to surprise him, not engage in a footrace if he decided to boogie on me. I walked casually to the edge of the yard and peered at the fence. But mostly at the yard. It was not a well-kept lawn. Mostly weeds and patchy brown and green grass. It did appear to have been mowed recently. There was no evidence of a dog. I was relieved. I like dogs and prefer not to have confrontations with any of them.

So, no dog. Maybe this wasn't a drug house, even though the yard and fence were common indications of higher than ordinary security. I hitched up my courage along with my pants, opened the gate and sauntered on in. I'd left my weapon in the car. Having a weapon handy sometimes led to unnecessary but lethal contretemps. I didn't see any curtains twitching to indicate a hidden watcher. Actually I didn't see any curtains at all on the four front windows. On the second floor, two windows looked out on the street and the shingled roof of the small porch. On the ground floor, two more slightly larger windows faced the street and the porch. They were dark, but had no shades. I approached the front door. The two mailboxes were empty. I'd noticed the mailman passing my car as he worked his way down the block. It was Wednesday, the traditional day when grocery store and other retail circulars were distributed, so someone in the house had already retrieved the delivery.

I found a doorbell and pressed it. I heard no sound. But that didn't mean much. After a reasonable interval I stepped to one side and pressed the bell again. Longer this time. Another pause. The neighborhood was quiet. I could faintly hear the constant background roar of the freeway several blocks away, part of the urban soundscape. Now I heard steps behind the door.

There came the rattle of a safety chain that didn't sound like one of those light-weight cheapies they sell to homeowners at your local hardware store or home improvement emporium. The door swung open quietly. It was a heavy door, probably steel-cored.

"Yeah?" The speaker was a heavy-set Latino who looked fat

at first glance, but was mostly bulked-up muscle. An iron-pumper, I figured.

"Harlan Ford?" I asked politely. Looking at the guy, something stirred far back in my memory archives. I couldn't come up with anything right then.

"Who's askin'?"

I fished out a business card and offered it. "Sean Sean, Investigations," I said. What? I should masquerade as an insurance salesman or something? Now something stirred behind the guy's eyes, but he just said, "What's your business with 'im?"

"Well, it's personal. Private like, so...." I gestured. "Is he in?" I said into the warm silence.

"I dunno."

"He does live here, right?"

The guy stared at me. I could tell he was trying to work something out in his head and it was taking serious effort.

"Uhhh. Maybe. Why you wanna see 'im?"

"Well, like I said, it's personal, as in private, you know? So I really can't discuss it with you. Do you know when he'll be back?"

That got a smile, sort of. It showed me his missing teeth, anyway. Or at least the gaps where a lot of his missing teeth had once resided. That helped. Now I knew I had encountered this bozo somewhere before. I just couldn't recall the details. Neither, apparently, could he.

Loud footsteps from behind mine host sounded as somebody wearing shoes with hard heels came toward the door on what must have been a bare wood floor.

Still unseen, the oncoming gentleman called, "Hey, Mel! Whoozatthdoor?" I recognized the voice.

Simultaneously several things happened. Harlan Ford appeared behind Mel—Melvin Harrison. Yeah, now I remembered who he was. Another thug I'd had a hand in putting in the slammer. Something about a chop shop on Minneapolis's near north side. I jumped forward to get around Harrison's bulk and grab Ford. He recognized me and his mouth fell open. He back-pedaled and turned on his heel to flee down the hall. Ford's heel slid a little and he tottered briefly.

Harrison hardly moved. He just raised one log-like leg and tripped me as I went by so I sprawled full-length onto the floor of the entryway. Then he moved. Before I could react, he sat on me, driving the air out of my chest. I couldn't get a breath, the edges of my vision began to darken and conscious thought began to slip away. Abruptly, the crushing weight on my back and butt was gone and I inhaled a massive, shaky breath. Still dizzy, I rolled toward the door and still heard the pounding but receding feet of my target as Ford made his escape. A door slammed back there somewhere at the rear of the building. I tried to get my feet under me, but things didn't work just right. I clawed at the wall, and my fingers slid across the rough paper-less plaster.

Then Harrison grabbed me by the waist and shoulder. His exhalation roared by my ear. "I got you now, you son of a bitch, Sean."

That was his mistake. Sitting on me his bulk had held me against the floor, but when he tried to turn me and haul me up so he could get at my face, I curled around his legs instead of resisting. My move took him just a little off balance for only a second or so but it was enough. I brought my legs up at the same instant and launched one knee into his groin as hard as I could manage. The resulting sharp expulsion of air and sudden slackening of Harrison's grip let me shift further out of his grasp. I didn't have as far to go or as much weight to handle so I was on my feet faster. He rose to one knee and grabbed for me. That was when I kicked him in the chest, wishing I was wearing boots instead of red tennis shoes. The look on his face was one of consternation as he slammed back against the door frame, shivering the front of the house with a solid thunk.

I kicked him again, this time smack in the jaw and he fell over, sliding limply down the wall. Harrison wasn't going anywhere anytime soon. Fortunately I was wearing soft soled hightops or I might have broken his face. I whirled and ran down the hall toward what appeared to be the back door. Halfway there I passed a closed door set off from the hallway. It flew open as I went past. Ford slammed the door at me, but his timing was off and he missed. I pivoted and swung a fist at his gut. It wasn't much of a blow but Ford stumbled backward, avoiding my follow-up swing, as I fell forward.

He tangled his feet and landed on the kitchen floor on one hip. I pounced on him, grabbed one arm and twisted it up behind his back. Raised it high enough so I could get to one knee and put some painful pressure on his wrist and elbow. The fight went out of him and he grunted. Most of these skells are too lazy to spend any time in the gym and their normal lifestyle didn't make for toned bodies. He was breathing heavily, puffing and wincing when I put a little more pressure on his elbow joint.

"Okay, okay. Jeeze. You don't have to break my arm."

"I didn't come after you with a piece of gas pipe, did I? Remember that incident in the Kavas' yard? Keep your head down," I snarled in warning. It was hard to sound menacing when I was still a little out of breath. I listened for a recovered Harrison as well. The chop shop deal in North Minneapolis had resulted in his collecting a few months in the workhouse because the County Attorney decided the evidence against him was too shaky for a GTA felony charge. It wasn't the sort of thing that would have Harrison looking for me, exactly, but he'd remember and want a shot at me when it was convenient. Right now I was vulnerable if he showed up here in his kitchen while I was trying to keep this miscreant subdued.

"I want to know who you're working for and everything you can remember about the deal with the Kavas."

That was as far as I got. There was a commotion at the other end of the kitchen. Another door apparently. It slammed open and mouth-breathing Harrison stormed in, carrying a baseball bat. I leaned on Ford's arm and he howled. "Later," I hissed at him. "This isn't finished."

I was outmanned and outgunned since I wasn't carrying. I bent back away from Ford who cried out at the extra pain, and dropped his arm, shoving him toward the advancing hulk. I wheeled and ran through the door back into the hall. Behind me Harrison howled in rage and tore after me. At least that's what it sounded like. I figured the two thugs expected me to head for the front door. So I ran the other way, toward the back of the house. As I slammed outside and sailed down the three steps into the yard, I heard a mild growl. The old dog lying on the back porch barely raised his head as I flew by.

I ran toward the alley and found an unlatched door in the wood fence that opened into the alley. I shut it quietly and slipped along the alley toward the end of the block. Behind me I could hear Ford and Harrison swearing at me and at each other. I turned the corner, walked swiftly to my car and quietly drove away. I'd have to find Mr. Ford at some later time when he was separated from Mr. Harrison.

Two blocks away, seeing no one following or even paying me any untoward attention, I drove around the block and cruised sedately past Harrison's house. There had been four vehicles parked on that block when I arrived, not including my own tired Taurus. One was a truck of uncertain ancient vintage with two flat tires which could therefore be discounted. None of the others had moved. That meant Ford was still in the vicinity or he was on foot. I'd noticed as I ran out of the back yard that the garage on the property contained no vehicle.

I drove down the block and as I turned right, in my side mirror I glimpsed a figure leave the Harrison place and start down the street away from me. From the size of him, it couldn't be Harrison and I'd had no indication of anyone else in the place. It looked like Ford was on the move. I turned right again at the next corner and idled up the street. I eased to a stop so I could see along the block and that was when my luck seemed to pick up. Here was Ford, all alone, coming toward me at a brisk pace. Looked like he was planning on putting some distance between himself and the Harrison place. Maybe he thought I'd called the cops. I left the car running and eased the driver's door open. Then I slid out, staying low and crab-walked around to the back of the vehicle, staying below window level, something that's easier for me than for a lot of folks.

I heard Ford slow and then stop. He must have been wearing leather-soled shoes and it was quiet in the neighborhood at the moment. He was probably looking around, wondering where the car's owner had got to. What an opportunity, he must be thinking. Steal the car, get out of the neighborhood, maybe find a new pad or even a new city.

He moved around the front of the car and grabbed the door handle. In one swift and, if I do say so, gracefully silent move I stepped behind him as he pulled the door open. He leaned down and started to enter my car. At that moment, I jammed the barrel of my small .32 into his back hard enough to leave a bruise and said, "Not a move, not even a flinch, or I'll blow away your kidney."

Ford knew from experience, I presume, the feel of a weapon in his side so he was instantly a good boy. No fight or flight action at all. He froze, one hand on the wheel, the other on the seat.

"Now, just put the right hand up on the wheel very slowly and sit. Then you slide across the seat and up against the passenger door. No sudden moves now. I have what's called an itchy trigger finger and I wouldn't lose any sleep over your death. There's a good boy. We're going to have a little conversation and then you can go on your merry way."

So far Ford hadn't made any sound except to hiss out his breath when he first felt the intrusion of the gun muzzle into his space. He obeyed, moving carefully and I followed. Once we were safely in the vehicle with the doors latched I relaxed. A little. I didn't want to have to deal with some inquisitive personal rights advocate or the cops called by an observant nosy neighbor. Now we were just two guys sitting in a car at the curb having a friendly chat. I kept the little gun at the ready. Not jammed into his side. It was too easy to grab or divert if you got a hand on it. I held it close to me as far from Ford as I could comfortably manage.

"Let's go back to our conversation in your friend Harrison's house there. Before the interruption. I just have a few questions. If you cooperate, we'll get outa here and no harm done. How long has Van Buren been your lawyer?"

"Coupla weeks is all."

"How'd you find him?" I wanted to know, because it didn't compute that this low-life in the seat next to me was even known to somebody like Van Buren who probably charged fees in the five figure per hour range. When he did pro bono work it was for a non-profit or cultural deal, not some bad-breath down at the heels skel like Ford. "Where'd you come into contact?" I asked again.

He shook his head. I never knew until yesterday he was my lawyer. I always talked to some kid, a Larry something. I don't rightly recall his last name."

That figured I thought. "So how did he even know about you? You got a rabbi in the system somewhere?"

That drew another blank and a shrug. I sighed. There was something going on here, just below the surface. It was like he braced for each question, then when the big one didn't come, he relaxed a little. I had the feeling I was inches away from some major answers, but didn't have enough info yet to ask the right questions. That would come. "So, spill. How'd you connect with Van Buren?"

"I had this thing in St. Paul, you know? Couple of years ago. I din't have no money. So the judge says he'll have somebody get in touch."

"A judge told you that."

"Right."

"And what was this thing you had?"

Shrugs. A little more tension. "Wasn't nothin' big. Just a B&E."

"Breaking and entering. What'd you get?"

"It was a bad rap. They hit me with a nickel at county."

"This wasn't your first go around, right?"

"Listen, what's this got to do with anything?"

"Mr. Ford. I tell you truth. I don't know right at the moment, but I'm going to figure it out. Trust me on this and when I do, if you're anywhere near ground zero, I'll be on you like a shark on a school of fry. Who was the judge?"

"When?"

"On the St. Paul case?"

"South St. Paul," he muttered.

"Who?" I yelled, startling Ford.

"I tole you I don't remember. Wait," he brightened momentarily. "I just remember it wasn't a real courtroom."

"Oh, really?"

"Yeah, really. It was in some big room, like a dining room, in a place up on a hill somewheres. I can't remember exactly, ya know?"

Bingo I thought. "Who else was there?"

"Hey how do I know? I don't remember stuff like that."

"But you and the judge weren't there alone, right?"

"No, man. I was in custody. There was a cop and there was a clerk or somebody making a record."

"A court reporter."

"Yeah, like that."

"Okay, Mr. Ford. Get out of my car and don't leave town."

With combustible eagerness Ford scrambled away from my little pistol, ran around the front of the car and headed in the same direction he'd been going when I intercepted him. I watched him go. The stink of his eagerness to get away lingered. Ford's skittishness didn't sit quite right. I had a feeling I'd let something get away from me. I went to my office to think about what I had learned and what I might have missed.

22

So, I thought, surveying my office, Ford was linked to my at-torney "friend," Van Buren, but it was a recent thing. I glanced around again while cogitating. It was a pleasant place to be at the moment, my office. Calm, sensible appearing. The warm late-afternoon sun sent slanting golden rays through the drifting dust motes. The Venetian blinds were half-closed and the air condition-ing in the building seemed to be working well. My office door was cracked open to signal there might be someone inside. I was expecting a potential client and I couldn't afford a secretary. Expe-rience had taught me that it was safer to keep some distance from strangers at the door. So instead of walking across the room and opening, possibly to the muzzle of a gun in the hands of some irate citizen, I'd holler "Come in," when someone knocked.

There was a firm, authoritative rap three times on the door jam and said door swung open a little farther.

"Yes?" I queried. A young, slender woman stood there. She looked hesitatingly toward me. I looked calmly back.

"Mr. Sean. My name is Lita, Lita Mason."

"Why don't you come in and tell me how I might possibly help you?" I stood up and gestured her toward the one unoccu-pied chair in the room. It's a chair set at a slight angle and toward one end of my rectangular heavy wooden desk. Ms. Lita Mason sank into the chair. It's one of those old-fashioned heavy types that wasn't too comfortable to be in for the long haul. If she tried to move it, she'd have no luck. I'd had it bolted to the floor a few years ago after an unhappy potential client tried to brain me with this chair's predecessor. Obviously that didn't happen, but I got the message and promptly made sure my office furniture was more secure.

Ms. Lita Mason didn't try to move the chair, she just sank gracefully into it. She smiled and then she didn't. A smile that was fleeting and seemed forced, sort of a social smile as if she'd been brought up to react this way in any situation. So I smiled back.

"You are lucky I was in," I said, "I don't spend a lot of time here in my office."

"I know. I've been waiting down the hall. Belinda Revulon is an acquaintance of mine."

"How can I help you?"

"My brother Tommy is missing."

"How long has he been gone?"

"Three days. I don't talk to him every day and my stepmother and I don't speak at all. He's been living with her."

"So what is it you would like me to do?"

"Find my brother, see what's up with him. Get him to call me. Or bring him home so I can talk to him."

"Three days is not very long and I take it he's an adult. He can pretty much go where he wants whenever he wants."

She nodded. "Yes, I understand. But he never does that. Leaves without any warning. No note, no call. Nothing. I'm really worried about him."

I sighed. Silently. I don't like these missing persons cases, mostly because I often end up being the messenger bringing bad news. Finding people who didn't want to be found and knew what they were doing wasn't impossible, but damn near so. I usually referred those seeking another to a large agency across town that had more resources than I. But for Belinda, I would make an exception. Besides if I knew the Revulons, they'd already done a ton of computer searches. If Tommy Mason had used a credit card or he'd done any of a number of things he'd be in the system and traces would be visible. There was, apparently, no trace. Zip. Nada.

Thomas Herbert Mason was tall, over six feet, blond and still in good shape, maybe 190 pounds his sister told me. He'd been a starring quarterback in high school and at thirty lost none of his swagger and self-assuredness. But he drank booze. In great quantities, upon too frequent occasions.

I got more particulars and a look at the small portrait she was carrying. I explained the financial arrangements and she promised to provide the material answers to several routine questions. I sent her down the hall to Belinda Revulon to get me several copies of the picture from their copy machine.

"While you're there, ask them to scan the picture into their computer. She was gone only a few minutes and then returned with the copies. We parted with a brief handshake and I started a file.

It appeared Tommy Mason had arisen three mornings ago as was his habit. He did the usual things, according to what Ms Mason told me her mother had related to her. Then he went out. And never returned. It happens I was somewhat familiar with Tommy Mason's neighborhood. It's in the lakes neighborhood on the western edge of Minneapolis. In my mind I re-created the scene. Tommy came out the front door and walked down the several steps to the sidewalk. There he turned either right or left on the sidewalk. If he went right and walked a block to the next corner, he then had a choice. He could cross the busy avenue to the bus stop that would deposit him downtown after a short ride. But why would he do that? Tommy Mason didn't have a car so he took the bus or someone drove him. If he stayed on the east side of the avenue, he could take a bus to the other end of the line, somewhere south of Fiftieth. But again, why would he do that?

If he walked the other way, he'd pass several well-kept homes in his neighborhood, ultimately ending in the park that surrounded Lake Harriet. Same question. Why? Maybe somebody picked him up in front of his place, or while he was walking one way or the other. I am a student of chance, of course. It sometimes helped in my line of work. And of unintended consequences. People often make un-reasoned choices, simple reactions to almost nothing which lead to other, unintended, actions or results. Some simple decisions, like whether to turn right or left at an intersection, result in earth-shaking changes in the life of the individual. Not always, of course. And if, for example, a decision to go right, rather than left, thus avoiding a runaway horse at the cliff edge, resulted in nothing discernable changing, the decision and its consequences went unremarked and, of course, unknown.

Tomorrow I would go walk Tommy Mason's neighborhood and try to detect any small or cosmic tremors that might lead me to finding Tommy. By tomorrow, Tommy might return all by himself.

Meanwhile, there was Harlan Ford. He'd been sentenced to the guideline stint in the county workhouse after pleading guilty to attempted breaking into a private domicile. There was no one home at the time and since Mr. Ford pleaded guilty, there was no formal prosecution, no courtroom. A simple routine with a retired judge was the usual routine. It saved the county money and time. And what retired judge had been taking such cases at the time? Turns out, it was a judge who just might be slightly bent, a judge who was on the lookout for the resources of a human kind such as an experienced felon who could be coerced into the occasional odd job on the other side of the law, for certain considerations, of course.

I would also, tomorrow, visit the South St. Paul courthouse and look at some old records. It would not surprise me in the least to learn that the retired judge in Mr. Ford's case, up in that room on the bluff overlooking the sweeping Mississippi River valley, was none other than my friend Judge George Polk.

Links, connections. Yes, I believed in links, and like carefully weaving a net, I was gradually finding links and connections between all the players, living and dead, connected to this case of the rusty revolver and a distant train robbery. The trick was to avoid being enmeshed in someone else's net. I would be the barracuda and slash through those alien nets to the ultimate prize; who ordered the deaths of Kent and Kristi Kava? And what had they to do with the stash in their back yard?

Without bothering to call, I drove up to the bluff in South St. Paul, to the slightly down-at-the-heels almost palatial home of the honorable George Polk (retired). I was again reminded that I had two George's in this case, George Van Buren, attorney at law and this judge. This time my knock on the door was answered promptly.

Upstairs, I once again sat across the big desk from his eminence. "I have agreed to see you again because I am intrigued by your efforts to make a great deal out of what by now must be beyond the memories of nearly everyone in the county."

"Your Honor, let me ask you about some of your recent activities after you left the bench. It's common in these litigious times, when court calendars become crowded, for retired judges to be called on to handle a limited number of cases, is that not true?"

"Yes, certainly. It's also a way for the city or county to avail itself of the accumulated years of experience and expertise of its judges, like myself, without saddling itself with the higher costs of sitting judges."

"You mean to say, I guess, that you only get paid for the work you do."

"Quite so."

"Do you use a particular courtroom? I ask, because I know some judges are particular about the arrangement of their courtroom. The physical arrangement, I mean."

"Oh, yes, that's quite common, actually. I never really minded the arrangement, you know so long as the chair was comfortable and the lighting was adequate."

"The lighting."

"Indeed. Early on I presided in some courtrooms in the old courthouse with no windows and just a few of what I might call early kerosene lamps."

Polk chuckled at what was apparently an inside joke of some kind. "We were also able to get out of the courthouse to what were sometimes called satellite facilities. Brought justice to the masses, in a manner of speaking."

"I wondered if you also occasionally held court on some of these cases in non-public facilities?"

Judge Polk frowned. "Hmmm. Well, now that you mention it, I did a few times. But only hearings, you understand. No actual trials. That would have been troublesome if not an outright violation, you see."

"But aren't all judicial proceedings pretty much meant to be in public?"

"Well, that's true. However there are some exceptions allowed by the laws of this state." The judge went on to explain things I already knew. Jury deliberations are secret. Sometimes judges hear procedural matters in chambers, things like that.

"I understand, Your Honor," I said, finally cutting him off. The atmosphere was getting a little thick. Maybe a lawyer like Scott Turow would put up with it, but I was getting impatient and I was already pretty sure this guy was bent. Outside the pale. Cheating. "So to summarize, you can recall a few times when you may have held hearings or procedural actions in private locations not normally used. Extra-judicial places, one might suggest."

"That would be correct."

"How about here, in your residence? Looks to me like you have adequate space."

Judge Polk frowned and looked introspective. At least that's how I interpreted the little glaze that appeared in his eyes. He might have just zoned out, for all I knew for sure. After a moment of silence he shifted and murmured, "Hmm. Well, yes. I believe I did that. Only once or twice. I confess I can't recall exactly, but there could have times when it was more expeditious for all concerned. Justice delayed is justice, denied, you know."

"Yes, sir, of course."

"However, I am sure there are adequate records of any such proceedings at the courthouse, should you require specific detail or a need to pursue this matter further."

"Yes sir, of course, but as you are probably aware, the city is only putting current proceedings on their computers. Your judicial activities would have happened prior to that, am I correct?"

Judge Polk nodded, a slight frown deepening the furrows in his high white brow. I was skating as close as I dared to his extra-judicial, probably illegal activities. I might need to talk with him again. So I wasn't quite ready to accuse him of law breaking to his face. But I now had almost irrefutable admission from the judge himself that he'd held sessions in his home, just as Harlan Ford had insisted.

I rose and made my goodbyes. Again the judge did not rise nor did he offer to shake my hand. It was more as if he was waving away a necessary but valueless underling. I suspected he thought that way about everybody around him. Again, information from Ford's eager-to-help interview while I held a gun to his chest, which didn't square at all with his aggressive behavior toward me when he tried to brain me with that piece of pipe at the Kava home.

Polk's almost silent woman-about-the-house led me to the front door, floating ahead of me down the long curving staircase in the gloom of the poorly lighted hallway. I left the seedy mansion with a feeling of relief. The pervasive gloom while I was inside seemed to have been an unseen weight on me, now lifted, as I walked slowly to my car through the waning heat of the day.

23

The next morning I went downtown to the Minneapolis PD to get started on my new case. The missing Tommy Mason. Naturally officialdom didn't have anything on him. That would have been too easy. Missing persons was devoid of any real help. Yes, they had a report on a Thomas Mason; missing since Thursday. Since I was not family, I wasn't going to get any additional information. I was lucky to get that much. That was O.K. I didn't need any information from officialdom that they hadn't already given me. All I really wanted to verify was that Ms. Mason was on the up and up; that she had, in fact, asked for official help. In another part of the high-rise government building, I talked to an acquaintance who was able to assure me that Tommy Mason had no arrest sheet and was not currently a person of interest, as the current jargon went. I even talked to a county contact. Same answer.

So far so good. I came out of the government building to the sound of a penny whistle and a guitar. The buskers were adept at the music they were offering and the pleasing notes swirled through the warm summer air.

Next stop, my office and Belinda Revulon. I opened the door to my office and the sound of the telephone buzzing. I grabbed the handset. It was Susan Polk. Her voice was high and rapid with anxiety.

"Mr. Sean! There are people here. They say they are from Family Services, or something like that."

"Why? What do they want?"

"They say they have an order. A court order or something."

"For what?"

"They say they're here to take Alex."

"Mrs. Polk. Stay calm. Where's Alex now?"

"He's still in school, but he'll be home in a little while. The bus will drop him right at the corner."

"All right. I'm coming out there right now. Answer their questions and try to seem cooperative, but don't say anything more than necessary. If Alex gets home before I get there try to stall them."

I broke the connection and dialed the White Bear Lake police department and asked for detective Stan Jackson. Wonder of wonders, he was at his desk.

Detective, somebody is at Alex Kava's aunt's. Susan Polk in Little Canada? Somebody is trying to nab Alex. Take him out of her home."

"What? I'll get the sheriff to send a car ASAP.

"Thanks, man. Tell 'em I'm on the way."

I dropped the phone and ran out. Jackson was being very cooperative, not asking a lot of useless questions, seemingly not worried about covering his ass. I guess smaller police forces are able to move with less bureaucracy than some larger units. Without endangering myself or anybody else—much—I made it to Susan Polk's without incident. I dialed it down at the corner and rolled decorously down the street. There was a tank in front of the house. Actually it was a black Cadillac Escalade SUV parked in the driveway blocking the sidewalk. I stopped behind the Caddy and got out, even though I was facing the wrong way on the street. A Ramsey County Sheriff squad was parked in front of Susan's house. It was facing the correct way.

I adjusted my shirt collar and walked briskly up the walk, still wondering how I was going to handle this situation. Nothing practical had occurred to me on the drive to Little Canada. I wasn't heeled and the idea of threatening these people with a gun had serious downsides. I stomped onto Susan Polk's porch. I tried to make plenty of noise, not so easy in soft-soled red tennis shoes. But I wanted to make my presence and my bone fides immediately known. Without bluster, projecting an authoritative sense of natural belonging sometimes carried the day. I turned the big brass knob and shoved the door open, knocking loudly with the other hand. I'd observed on my earlier visits that she didn't always keep her door locked.

"Susan," I called, "it's Sean Sean."

"Mr. Sean," came an immediate strong response. "We're in the living room." It didn't sound as if Ms. Polk was feeling intimidated.

I followed her voice and walked in as if I had every right in the world to be there. The deputy sheriff was standing to one side, hands at his waist in a decidedly non-belligerent stance.

"What's up?" I demanded, looking at the three strangers also standing in a small group in the center of the room. They were behind a low coffee table. On the couch, Susan Polk sat, back straight, knees together, hands clasped in her lap. She looked upset, but in a determined, centered sort of way, as if she wasn't about to concede much of anything to anybody. She'd decided to see this through. Whatever 'this' was.

I raised my eyebrows and stared at three well-dressed strangers. "Who's this?"

The woman, dark, shorthaired, in a deep blue tailored power suit, looked back at me. A moment's hesitation, then she said calmly. My name is Elissa Clinton. From Children and Family Protection Services. This is my assistant, Jed Meese, and Mr. Lott, a private investigator."

I ran Lott through my mental database. Nothing came up.

"We have come to take Alex Kava into protective custody."

"For what purpose?"

She seemed slightly aggrieved that I had asked. "Mr. Sean, the boy is a possible witness to a double homicide. He needs protection."

"From whom? The White Bear Lake PD has primary jurisdiction and they immediately put Alex in custody of his aunt, right? He's been available for interviewing right along. So what's the sudden change?"

Of course I knew prosecutors could have abrupt changes of attitude, depending on what information was developed as the case went along, but so far as I was aware, nobody had yet been charged. I had a feeling something was hinky here. I was going to ask a lot of questions, stalling, delaying and trying to come up with something that would keep Alex out of their clutches.

"I'm not aware you have any status here, Mr....Sean." Clinton was trying to reassert her authority, feeling momentum ebbing away from her now that the deputy and I had arrived on the scene. Her hesitation over my name was interesting. I wondered if Susan Polk had given the woman my full name. I hadn't offered Ms. Clinton my card and wondered if Susan Polk had explained that my first and last names were identical. Why would she? Had Clinton foreknowledge of the situation? Had she been warned to watch out for me? A small thing, perhaps, but kingdoms have been lost for want of a nail, right? People often hesitate because my first name is the same as my last. I wondered if this woman had been briefed and knew my connection to Alex. If so, by whom?

"I'm not aware you have any status here, Ms. Clinton. Do you have a paper of some kind?" Maybe this was just a case of a concerned social worker overstepping her authority. I stuck out a hand. At the same time I glanced at Susan. She shrugged and rolled her eyes as if the whole scene was off kilter.

Ms. Clinton smiled a cold grimace at me and whipped a folded paper in a blue cover sheet out of her small case. She thrust it at me. I nodded, graciously, I thought, and took it from her outstretched fingers. The sheriff's deputy shifted his stance and his equipment belt creaked the way good leather does. I glanced up and saw the man they'd called Lott had shifted to one side so he could see out the front window while also settling farther to my right side. It was a good move, in the event I was carrying a weapon and was right handed, which I wasn't. Lott had moved so if I drew on him I'd have to sweep a pistol in a farther arc to line up an accurate shot at him. In situations like this one, a few extra microseconds could be an advantage. Lott had seen me using my right hand to gesture and to reach for the paper Ms. Clinton was offering. So he assumed I was right handed. Ergo, if I was wearing a shoulder holster, I'd have it in my left armpit. Cross drawing was always a little faster, although we were a long way from a shooting situation.

Lott had made an erroneous assumption.

I unfolded the paper and scanned it. As I'd expected, it was a legal document of some sort. The deputy creaked again and I saw him shifting slightly in a counter move to Lott's. Oh good. It reassured me a little, but I hoped these two cowboys didn't get too tense. Gunplay in this room wouldn't solve anything. I saw Lott hunch his shoulders and then he slowly moved his hands away from his waist, turning his palms outward in a sign of surrender. Good.

The document Clinton had given me was a writ, a legal order signed by a judge, authorizing the removal of a person named Alex Kava, a minor, to the custody and protection of the court of South St. Paul. It appeared proper, but what did I know? The unusual aspect that occurred to me was lack of notice to Susan Polk, since there had been no contention that she was unfit to care for the boy. Why removal to South Saint Paul? It is usual for such writs to be handled by the sheriff's department in whatever county has jurisdiction. Why wasn't a Ramsey County deputy serving the order instead of helping me to stall these people? Then there was this other thing. Judge George Polk had signed the writ.

24

I politely explained that I didn't think they had the right to remove Alex, since the lawmen in charge of the murder investigation still had primary jurisdiction and they hadn't been notified. The unhappy trio from CPS left, darkly promising to follow up on the situation. Alex's situation. That's what the woman called it. I wondered why she didn't call it Alex's circumstances. Was that CPS-speak for something else? A code? I didn't have time to figure it out. I had to move my car before they rammed their big black Escalade into my inoffensive little blue Taurus. The woman stared at me while I maneuvered out of their way as if she was trying to be sure she wouldn't forget what I looked like. Well, good luck to her, I thought.

When I parked in a more legal position, I nodded goodbye to the deputy sheriff who was also leaving. I spotted Alex Kava sauntering down the street toward us. He'd just gotten off the school bus at the corner. He had a smile on his face and he looked even happier when I stopped and waved to him. "Hey, Alex, how'zit goin' pal?"

He tugged my hand and we turned up the steps to his home. "Great, Mr. Sean. My teacher says we have to be careful with our words and always say the "g" at the end of ing."

I nodded. "All right, I'll try to do better at that." The boy released my hand and zipped across the porch and into the house calling for his dog. Susan met me as I climbed the last step to the porch.

"Do you think they'll come back and try to take him again?"

"I doubt it. And I'm going to make some calls to try to see to it you and Alex are left alone. I don't think this was a legitimate effort. The judge who signed the order may be involved in this whole thing right up to his judicial collar. I'm just not sure how or how much, but I will find out. Meantime, I'll make sure the judge knows I'm onto his game."

I called goodbye to Alex and left Little Canada.

On the road I thought about driving out to South St. Paul to see the judge again but then I decided a threatening phone call would be just as effective. I planned to call and snarl at him. Intimidation, that was the key at this point. At the same time realized that I might have contributed to Alex's possible exposure by the games I was playing. I figured by now there must be a level of chatter about the pistol the BCA was supposedly working on. Had that chatter provoked this move by the judge?

Back home again, though not in Indiana, I called Detective Jackson out in White Bear. "Hey, Sean NMI Sean," he chortled. "My favorite PI. What can we do for you this fine day?"

"For starters I appreciate your getting a deputy sheriff to Susan Polk's so promptly. I assume you've been advised of the results?"

"All in a day's work serving the taxpayer."

"Can you give me any news or progress about finding the killers."

Jackson lost his joviality instantly. "I wish I had something to talk about. Hell, I wish I had some rumor to deny. I take it your conversations with the boy weren't much help."

"I think we've got everything he has. In fact I'm sure of it. I did want to be sure you knew that the judge who signed the removal order is that retired judge I told you about earlier, George Polk."

"Seems to me he's getting pretty active for a retired judge."

"That was my impression, too. I was going to call him and

threaten him. Now I've decided that might be a bad idea."

"Yeah. Why don't I call the city? I know a few people down there. Maybe I can get a handle on what's going on."

"These were county folks. I have nothing that says they're part of some big conspiracy."

"I hear you. But if I put a bug in somebody at the city level, that might get me or somebody else a shot at county where I have fewer contacts. We can talk about inter-agency cooperation, you see."

"I do see, thanks." Privately I didn't think the detective could help much in this matter and I didn't have any solid contacts with the county welfare system which is where PS was housed. I needed to figure out a way to isolate Alex from any potential danger. I could get him a discreet bodyguard, but that had problems of its own making, apart from the financial aspect. The best thing I could do was to solve the damn case and see the killer of his parents in custody. In the meantime, maybe I would see about some discreet protection.

* * * *

Like a lot of P.I.s you read about I have friends. None of mine are stone killers like Bolitar's. You may also have noticed that I try to stay on the friendly side of the cops in my bailiwick. I find that a lot easier than fighting with them all the time. That way we occasionally help each other out. Here, though, I decided I wanted some extra-judicial watching. I know a couple of ex-pro wrestlers. They make an impressive display when necessary. So I got on the horn and hired two retired heavyweights. They don't move very fast—knee problems you see, but they'd be alert and make their intimidating selves known if necessary.

Then I called Susan Polk and let her know about my move. I explained that she shouldn't be alarmed at two hulks lurking about in her bushes from time to time. Three quick calls set up a dawn to dusk watch. Then I leaned back in my chair, put my feet on the desk and reviewed the known facts. The kid's dog found a stash of money and a rusty revolver next to the old garage Alex's dad was rebuilding. The stash appeared to have been a temporary burial, and was probably part of the money taken during the great train robbery of 1933 in South St. Paul. That led me to suppose that at least one of the gang of robbers had died or been imprisoned before he could get back and retrieve the boodle.

Before the discovery of the stash, several people with no obvious legitimate interest in the renovation project had shown up at the Kavas'. That said to me somebody or several somebodies had some foreknowledge of and perhaps unhealthy interest in the property. Now there was something to follow up. I made a note. We detectives do that sometimes, although I occasionally wonder about the detectives in the novels I read. Most of them must have prodigious memories because they never seem to write anything down. Or dictate memos, or call in their good-looking secretaries to take dictation while the detective ogles the woman's legs. I, on the other hand, don't have a secretary. I make notes and I've had my files ripped up a couple of times. Now I have files on a computer server, it's called. Never mind where. Actually, I couldn't tell you where. I've never seen it—the server. I don't even know if it's real. The Revulons, who set this all up, assure me it's real and legitimate and when I forget the access codes, I call Betsey or Belinda. They're like big sisters in addition to being my expert computer advisors.

I also have hand-written notes stashed outside the office in concealed files. Just in case. Anyway, first comes the revolver, then the decomposed cash, then I start poking around. The ancient trail leads me to the Railway Express robbery. The Kavas are murdered and I make a visit to the cop shop in South St. Paul, which results in the shooting death of detective McKinley on the street.

Then there's that really weird ploy by our distinguished local attorney George Van Buren. He left his grandkid along a lake trail for me to find and "rescue." Just so he'd have a legitimate (to him) reason to contact me. And what I got out of that contact was that Harlan Ford was a client of his and that I should focus on the revolver as the linch pin of the case.

So here I was in the middle of a case with too many players. Give me a simple workman's comp fraud anytime. One insured (usually) and one insurer. Question, legitimate claim or not? Dig up or surveil the evidence. Write and submit report. End of story. Submit bill, cash check and move on to the next bad guy. This business was another kettle of fish altogether.

I'd spent a week on this case and I didn't feel I was significantly closer to solving it than when Alex and his dad had first shown up in my office with that damn revolver. That revolver. I needed to do some more digging in that direction. Maybe there were unsolved gunshot-related crimes around the time of the robbery. A real long shot but what the Hell.

I called South St. Paul and asked for Chief Johnson. After I gave the woman who answered my name, my address, my reason for calling and the brand and color of my under shorts, she put me through to his eminence, Chief of Police Andrew Johnson.

"Mr. Sean, what progress on the killing of my detective?"

"Some, sir. I seem to be narrowing the field of suspects."

"Good, good. My homicide squad seems to be also moving forward at a steady pace. What can I do for you today?"

What? I thought. Are we having a race to see who gets to the brass ring first? "I'm trying to determine if the revolver I found has any history of criminal activity around the time of the great Railway Express robbery."

"Yes, yes, I see. Well, I think this may be a waste of time but I can assign someone to check the files. Give me your parameters."

"Thanks, Chief, I won't forget this. I'm looking for any evidence of a crime involving a handgun where the weapon was fired and there's something in your files. I think we can restrict the time frame to a period between 1930 and 1934."

"Hmm. Probably a lot of work. We won't ever be sure we've found every case, but I guess it's worth a shot. I'll get somebody on it right away," he said.

I didn't hold out much hope. The weapon could have been used in a robbery at the other end of the state or in another state altogether, for that matter. But it was a thread, something to follow up. If the whole case went south at least I could say we tried.

25

Meanwhile, back at the office, I had this missing person, Tommy Mason. I needed to spend some energy and time on this job. From his sister I had a list of friends and places where he sometimes hung out. I went to the places first on the theory that I'd encounter more folks at each stop. Bars, social clubs. Restaurants. I taxied down town to the Galway Bar and Grille. It was a place I sort of knew, a pseudo-Irish pub in the "auld style," doncha know. The operators occasionally staged events of live music or bad poetry readings. A former member of the legislature and a failed candidate for president had performed there. The bartender, when I came through the massive wood paneled door, was a comely lass of about six feet with a nice figure and what looked like muscles on top of normal muscles under the sleeves of her white blouse. Her hair was shoulder length, sort of dark blonde. She wore it loose and streaked. The tiny wrinkles around her eyes when she smiled a welcome at me indicated she'd been on this earth for a few years.

"What can I get you this foine day?"

"Faith, 'tis a sight for me tired eyes, you are, an' I'll have a nice glass of your best ale, if you please."

We both laughed at our bad Irish accents. She went about the business of finding me a clean, appropriately shaped glass, and, after rejecting the first, poured a neat and generous drink of the house ale. I asked, but I didn't recognize the label. The Irish also make a fine whiskey to which I'm sometimes partial, but this early I figured I needed to keep a clear head.

"I'm looking for a man goes by the name of Tommy Mason. My information from his sister is that he sometimes favors this establishment."

"Ah, an Orangeman would he be?"

"I have no idea, nor does it matter to me what he is, other than apparently, at the moment, missing. 'Tis a matter of some concern to his sister." I took the small picture from my breast pocket and slid it across the polished wood bar toward her. She leaned over and peered at it as if she might be nearsighted and too vain to wear glasses or contacts.

While she examined the photo, I glanced around. Since the passage of smoking bans in Minneapolis, bar atmospheres had gotten a lot cleaner but they'd lost that certain smelly and dingy ambiance. All to the good. The atmosphere above traditional mean streets that are trod upon by skells and investigators needn't be always nasty or inherently dangerous to one's health. Bullets, knives, guns and clubs were enough to deal with.

I sipped my ale and returned my attention to the bartender. She extended one long slender finger and pushed the picture back toward me. "Well, sir, he looks familiar, that I will admit. And he was probably in here last week sometime."

"Day? Night?

She nodded. "Had to have been an afternoon. I work from about ten to three."

"Anything else?"

She shook her head. "Nope. Sorry. I smiled, finished my drink, placed a nice tip in her tip jar and sauntered out. On to the next place, a few blocks over and definitely down. Minneapolis no longer has what one would call a skid row, which it did whilst I was growing up hereabouts. Then there were seedy strip joints, cheek by jowl with so-called adult theaters, those that catered mainly to juvenile male fantasies. I don't mind admitting I'd been in a few during my callow youth. Never mind. There were flop houses and plain vanilla bars all sort of smooshed together in about a sixteen-block area. It was called the Gateway in those days. Just a couple of short blocks from the river and St. Anthony Falls. Immigrant laborers who worked on the nearby railroads and in the many flour mills along the river lived in the district, along with prostitutes, bad guys and other ordinary poor folk. They all jostled and strained together in the Gateway. Along with a posh hotel, a few good office buildings and an occasional true historic relic.

In Minneapolis, unlike St. Paul across and down river a bit, folks in charge believed in a clean sweep when it came to something called urban renewal. So they took out the Gateway, pretty much all of it, and built a bunch of modern glass and steel and concrete buildings, parking ramps and enclosed skyways to connect them. Historical building preservation was largely akin to swearing in the presence of women in those years.

So now the bad folk in Minneapolis, instead of being mostly concentrated where the cops could keep an eye on them, were scattered in smaller enclaves here and there about the downtown and the rest of the city. Downtown, or the Loop as they call it in Chi town, is a mixed gaggle of upscale and medium scale restaurants, hotels, parks, cultural icons and such like. Not long ago somebody wanted to put an upscale titty bar in a new entertainment complex right smack-dab on Hennepin Avenue there. Caused a bit of an uproar. Nobody seemed to worry too much about the topless place up the street a couple of blocks where some of the city's finest—and I'm not referring to police—tend to congregate.

Ace's Dance Palace it was called. A few girls who didn't seem to have much rhythm but knew where to find the clasp on their bras, paraded listlessly around a space elevated behind the bar. Large bartenders stood in front of you at the bar. They blocked your view if you weren't drinking, or were downing watered drinks too slowly. All in all a really welcoming place. It was next on my list. At this time of day it was not crowded and there was only a single lonesome female swaying gently on the runway. She was small, thin, with tiny breasts and no discernable pubic hair, not that I looked too closely.

The bartender was the usual large surly edition. I asked about Tommy Mason and he said he hadn't seen anybody by that name. Ever.

I importuned him and beseeched his memory with a Benjamin, exposed in my fingers. He peered closely at the picture and finally grunted that he might have seen the guy, but had no memory of when that might have been. We jousted for a few minutes and in the end I left the hundred on the bar and went out of the bar itself. The naked girl didn't smile and didn't stop her listless swaying.

I spent the rest of the day and into the early evening sipping inexpertly mixed drinks or sucking on cold bottles of beer, leaving a trail of currency, showing the picture, and asking the same question over and over again. All too little or no avail. A few people had seen Tommy in the past couple of days, most had not or couldn't or wouldn't remember him. All in all, it was a fruitless and depressing episode.

I was about to give it up for the night, having exhausted Ms. Mason's list of public venues, but since I was outside one of the only up-scale gay nightclubs in the area, I decided to give it a go. Not that there had been any indication that Tommy Mason was gay. But the Gay Nineties had a reputation for staging periodic classy shows. This was such a period. The signs outside invited passersby to enter and see a top drag queen comedian and a Spectacular Revu.

So, what the Hell? I said Hello to the woman in the tiny ticket booth just inside the front door, who, it turned out, I was acquainted with. She recognized the picture and said he came there often.

"Is it possible Mr. Mason might be inside?"

"Yes," said she, "it is possible. I haven't seen him tonight but I haven't been on duty the whole evening, either. Just don't disturb the customers."

I went inside and made my way through the bar to the show room. The place had been remodeled, if that's the word, since my last visit. A stage large enough to accommodate a small band of two or three with a piano and also room for a dancer or comedian or whatever had been added. Red and blue spotlights played in moving circles on the stage and back wall. The concrete block wall behind the stage was largely covered with some kind of tatty red velour drape. The drape or curtain also concealed the entrance to the basement. It looked to me like the performers entered and exited through a slit in the drape directly to the head of the stairs. I thought about it and recalled the layout from previous visits.

Folding chairs were arranged around two sides of the stage in ragged rows set close together. It made for a difficult time getting in or out, once the already dim house lights were extinguished in favor of the rudimentary stage lights.

I looked over the room, which was almost empty. Only a few patrons in widely scattered chairs patiently waited for the show to begin. The trap set on the stage was smaller than many drummers use. He didn't need a lot for a house this tiny. Even so, if he really got going on the two cymbals, the snare and the small bass drum, the sound would be heard all the way into the street.

I had a brief chat with the second bartender, a man I knew as a former client. He waved off the manager who obviously wanted me to move away from the doorway as more patrons of the show went into the room.

A female impersonator I had seen before appeared beside me. "See anything you like, sweetie?" he said. He was a tall dude, over six feet, I judged. Of course most people over five-five look tall to me.

"I'm not a customer," I said tersely, concentrating on the faces of the men. I fished the picture out of my pocket and offered it.

"Oh, you lookin' for Tommy Mason? He's a regular here, but you know he's straight?"

I didn't care one way or the other. His sister hadn't mentioned it so I had assumed that if he went to gay establishments, he was like some straight men, curious about the gay population, or interested in the entertainment. My job was to find the man and try to get him to call his sister. "Have you seen him recently? Like yesterday or today?"

"No, sorry. If I see him, do you want to give him a message?"

"Yeah, tell him to call his sister."

"That's it?"

"That's it." I started to turn away.

"OK. You come on back now, short stuff."

I raised a hand as I headed back toward the street entrance, scanning faces as I went and not seeing my target. It was getting late and I had other irons in the fire. Time, my feet were telling me, to get prone. It was too late to disturb Catherine, so I taxied to my office, found my Taurus and drove on home to Roseville planning for a dip in my hot tub and a quiet restful night.

26

I called the Hennepin County office of Missing Persons again, just in case there'd been a development. There was none. Then I called a woman I knew casually who worked in the PD across the river. She got back to me after an hour to assured me there was no Tommy Mason in the system. That is, he wasn't in jail, there weren't any warrants pending, he wasn't a person of interest in some hanging case.

The list his sister had supplied me of possible hangouts included a few in St. Paul. I'd already checked Minneapolis so it was on to The Saintly City. Daytime perambulating on Grand or Seventh in downtown is fairly easy because there aren't the crowds. That was especially true since a recent action by the local boys in blue had swept up a number of skells in the retail drug business who drew crowds to certain bus stop locations. After weeks of surveillance, arrests had been made, substantially reducing loitering traffic at several locations.

I dropped in at Joe's Bar on Seventh. I know, I know, but that's what it's named. It was cool and quiet and the bartender, a gent of about sixty, served me an icy mug of Heilemans Old Style Lager. It tasted mighty fine. Yes, he told me, he knew Tommy Mason, although he hadn't seen him in a while. Why did I inquire?

"He seems to be missing and his sister is worried. He hasn't been gone all that long, but, as I say, his sister is worried. So I'm looking."

"Well, sir, I think he was in here a couple of nights ago. I remember because he got into it with one of the regulars, fella named Raymond Polk."

"That a fact." My mind raced. Could this be the same Ray Polk I had been looking for? The one who had apparently skipped out on that landlord with bad breath? When I thought about it I realized that I was only a couple of blocks from that very rooming house. "Serious altercation?" I asked.

"Naw. They were both a little drunk. I let 'em whale away at each other for a few minutes. Sorta diffuse their anger, if you know what I mean."

"Any idea what happened to this Polk fellow? Reason I wonder is, I'd like to ask him a couple of questions about another case I'm working on."

"Happens I do," smiled my friendly bartender. "He's sitting in the back booth there. Been here all afternoon."

I swiveled around on my stool and looked to the back of the barroom. There was a man sitting there in the last booth right beside the door marked MEN, just as the bartender said. He appeared to be doing nothing out of the ordinary. He had long dark hair and when he lifted his glass I could see it was almost empty.

"What's he drinking?"

"Old Style, same as you."

"Pull me another glass and give me a refill, if you please."

I paid and carried the two brimming glasses with just the right sized heads back to Polk's booth. I slid in and plunked a glass in front of him. Polk looked at the full glass, flicked his eyes at me and nodded his thanks once.

"Something I can do for you?"

"Possibly. You had a disagreement with Tommy Mason the other night?"

"Yes, as it happens." He grinned briefly. "We took a couple of swings at each other. No damage done. Is there a problem?"

"No. I've been trying to find him though. Mind telling me what the fight was about?"

Polk took a long swallow and emptied most of the fresh glass. "Politics. He likes the mayor an' I don't. We got a little insulting with each other."

"You know a South St. Paul judge named Polk?"

"Sort of. I know of him."

"Any relation?"

"None that I am aware of. Every so often I get asked that, usually in here. Some of Jake's customers have occasional trouble with the law. They wonder if I have any influence over there. I don't. Far as I know, we aren't related in any way."

"How about a Kristi Polk?"

Again a negative shake of his shaggy head. "Nope. Never heard of her."

Another dead end. "Let's get back to Tommy Mason. How well do you know him?"

"Hardly at all. Fact is, he's like me, somebody who likes the way Jake serves his beer. I'm in here a good deal and I run into Tom. We discuss the affairs of the world from time to time." He shrugged. "That's about it. Mind telling me why this interest in Mason?"

I shrugged in return. "Nothing special. I have a message from his sister is all."

"Ah, would that be Lita? He's mentioned her a couple of times. You might try some of the other places along Seventh. I've seen him in one or two."

"Thanks." I rose and made my way past the bartender through the still almost empty bar and back to the street. I turned right and headed down the avenue to the next bar. It looked to stretch out to be a long afternoon and evening. Unless I got lucky.

* * * *

I didn't get lucky so later in the night I headed on home feeling a little bloated from the beer. I didn't drink all that much but it was a long succession of joints. I also realized I could just turn around and go back east to the same places again, where I might very well encounter the elusive Mr. Mason, or not. I went to Roseville instead.

There were no messages of any interest on my answering device so I hit the sack after a few minutes of horseplay with the cats. The morning would bring a fresh new day and I might just have an inspiration.

Fortunately nothing disturbed my night and after a brisk walk around the lake I called Catherine to make plans for dinner that evening. Next on my agenda was a call to Lita Mason. The tenuous connection between Tommy Mason and Raymond Polk, who apparently had no connection to my Judge Polk still bothered me. A little. There was probably nothing to it but that's something we detectives try not to ignore. In most cases there are numerous dead ends or leads that go nowhere, or questions left unresolved after the mystery is solved. Some people I know worry such loose ends until they either go away or dissolve. Sometimes they fade through lack of attention. A detective gets busy with new cases.

This Raymond Polk connection to Tommy Mason was probably one of them. Like the business of the harassing calls to Catherine. They undoubtedly had no connection to me, nor was the attempt by CPS to take Alex away from his aunt, Susan, anything but a routine screw-up. However, I would try to follow-up.

So I called Lita.

"I was wondering, Ms. Mason, if Tommy has a record with the police? Has he been arrested? Charged with anything? Even a traffic ticket."

Silence on the line while she thought. "There have been a few incidents. Fighting, public drunkenness. Nothing major that I'm aware of. Tommy wouldn't necessarily tell me. There was an incident in South St. Paul a few months ago. Tommy was in jail overnight and the judge let him go with just a warning because Tommy was just defending himself. That's the usual pattern. Tommy will say something provocative. The argument will escalate and then somebody takes a swing at Tommy so he defends himself. He boxed a little in high school so he's pretty good with his fists when he's provoked."

"Do you recall the name of the judge?" A tiny bell was ringing in my mind.

"Sorry, no. I'm not sure I ever knew. Does this help?"

"It may. I'll be in touch."

Poking through the state databases of police activity, a friend of mine discovered that Tommy Mason had a short history of minor infractions as a result of which the cops were sometimes called to make peace before things got entirely out of hand. Reading between the lines, my friend advised me that the police patrols in both cities had Mason in their sights as a perennial if minor troublemaker.

However, I was pleased and interested to learn that his fractious nature had carried him into South St. Paul as well. I might very well have seen Mason's name when I went through some of Judge Polk's case records at the courthouse, but until I'd interviewed his sister, it wouldn't have meant anything to me. Now I was wondering if Tommy Mason was one of the men the judge had used or tried to use for his illegal activities.

27

I woke early that morning with Tommy Mason on my mind. It was just coincidental that his sister came to see me about finding him at a time when he might have been entangled with the Kava and McKinley murders. The fact that Mason seemed to have done a runner when the judge was looking for folks on the wrong side of the law to assist him, maybe said he was trying to do the right thing. If he was absent when the judge put out a call, he couldn't be faulted for not showing up, right?

During my perambulations of the cities hot spots I'd made sure the word began to circulate that I would be receptive to information about Mr. Mason from most any source. Like most P.I.s I have a small coterie of snitches, boys and girls on the periphery of the underworld who are not averse to making a few extra coins by repeating what they know. Cops now call them confidential informants or CIs. I guess it's more polite than calling them snitches. Whatever their label, they sometimes provided useful gossip. Sometimes not.

There was a terse message on my answering device when I checked my machine. The voice was obviously altered and he or she left no name. In the past I would have learned, sometimes through tortuous means, that so-and-so wanted to meet me in some secluded rendezvous, where I'd pass crumpled bills to a sweaty palm for a few whispered words. You see it in a lot of gangster and detective movies.

In the modern era electronics plays a bigger part. I often got information via the telephone and later encountered the purveyor so I could make a pay-off. I always paid, and the other party always knew I would. Otherwise valuable sources of information, the lifeblood of a successful P.I. business dried up.

So, one of my snitches had called to tell me where he thought Tommy Mason could be found. The problem was, the location he gave me was outside my territory. Sixty miles outside, in Hutchinson Minnesota. Hutchinson is a nice little town I've only been through one time while on my way to somewhere else. I had no desire to drive out there but the message had been pretty explicit. I didn't know anybody in the PI biz, or in Law Enforcement either, in that part of Minnesota. But I went.

Took me the better part of two hours to wend my way through the cities and out along the lakes and green valleys of the area. I got to Hutchinson in good order and went to the local police station. I almost always do that in case of a future dust-up. The uniform at the desk didn't seem to mind or care. He took my card. He said he knew of the down-at-the-heels rooming house I sought. Then he wished me good luck and I sauntered out into the sunshine.

I found the aforesaid rooming house on the southern edge of town. It was on a small lot littered with what looked like tall weeds and unidentifiable auto parts. There was no garage. The lot backed up to a single-story concrete block building that had once sheltered a service station and auto repair shop.

Down-at-the-heels doesn't begin to adequately describe the place. It was a two-story unpainted cube, just about as high as it was wide and deep. It sat in the middle of the lot and it needed maintenance. I drove by once, turned a block and motored back to a corner where I could park and watch for a time. There were four windows on the front, plus the door. On the sides—I saw both on my drive by—there were also four windows, two up and two down. No door. There had to be one on the back. Two of the windows on this side had room air conditioners hanging slightly askew in the frames.

I watched for about half an hour. No one entered and no one left. So I got out, locked the car and went across the street and up the cracked concrete walk. The door was up three steps under a tiny weather roof. It was ajar. At least it wasn't latched. I pushed it open and walked into a narrow hallway.

I suspected this place had once been a single family home, later altered. On my immediate right was a door. Opposite it was another almost identical door. Ahead of me was a steep narrow stair that obviously ascended to the second floor. On the wall beside the door on my left were six battered black metal mailboxes. They were separately nailed to the wall by a single nail through the flange at the top of each box. At one time there had been names on the boxes. Now there were dingy pieces of masking tape. Someone had written a number on each. One through six.

When I walked down the hall a short way, the floor creaked loudly. Under the stairs I saw another door. No label, like the other doors in view. But I'd bet a sawbuck that door led to the basement. I tried the handle. It wasn't locked and swung open on well-oiled hinges. Right. Stairs to the basement. The hall atmosphere carried a mixture of old and new cooking odors and musty air.

I turned around and squinted in the dimness from the light cast by the CFL screwed into an overhead socket. Nothing for it, I stood close and rapped on the first door to the left of the front door. That placed me with my back to the stair, but out of sight of anyone on the second floor unless they came down several steps. It also placed me with my back to the door on the other side of the narrow hall. I faced the door on which I rapped. My cop-rap was loud. The building was silent. I rapped again. Then I heard noises from the door behind me.

I pivoted and waited. Two more locks were undone, judging by the sounds and the door silently opened. An old man in a white undershirt and raggedy shorts and bare feet looked at me. He was shorter and older than I am by quite a lot.

"He ain't home. Got 'im a temporary job."

"Do you know this man?" I said sternly in my best imitation-cop voice, sticking my photo of Tommy Mason in his face.

He pulled back a bit and looked intently at the photo. "Yep. That's Tommy Mason."

"Seen him recently?"

"Yes. You just missed him. He's been bunking with me for a few days."

I opened my mouth to ask another question but the man raised his hands and went right on. "He's a distant relative. I run into him couple of times a year. Usually he comes out here to see me. Sometimes he stays, sometimes not. Never been in any real trouble. He left this mornin'. Early."

He took a breath and I asked, "Do you know where he went?"

Old man shook his head and said, "Tommy didn't have no car so he musta been planning to hitch somewhere."

Rats, another dead end. "If he gets in touch, tell him to call his sister, Lita. She's worried."

The old man shrugged and nodded. I offered him a fin for disturbing him and he backed up. "Nope, forget it. I got my pension and social. You don't owe me nothing."

I didn't want to offend him further so I put the money away and thanked him. Then I left. It was clear that I had hit another dead end. Even if I canvassed the town from end to end chances of finding someone who saw Mason and where he went this morning were unlikely at best. I drove home.

28

The telephone rang at two. Dammit, why couldn't people in crisis manage to call during normal hours? It was pitch black out. Normal this time of night. But I suppose that's part of why I became a private investigator. No streetlight broke the gloom outside my window. My thoughts were a little scrambled, it being the second of those low-number witching hours the fantasy writers are always going on about. The voice at the other end of the line, or the satellite, I suppose, was hoarse and halting.

"Mr. Sean?"

"Yeah," I said. "That's what I was named when I hit the sack a few hours ago. Why are you calling at such an ungodly time?"

"I heard you were looking for me."

"That depends on who you are." Long pause, like the guy was trying to decide whether to go on or end it. The call.

"Yeah. You were in Hutch today. My name is Tommy. Tommy Mason."

The caller's name cleared the sleep from my brain and I sat up in bed, the receiver pressed to my ear. "This Tommy Mason I'm talkin' to?" I muttered.

"Yeah that's me. I hear you are looking for me. Can I ask why?"

"Sure you can. Your sister, Lita. She contacted me, wanted me to find you since apparently you've been out of touch a few days. She's worried about you."

Long sigh. I heard traffic in the background, but faintly. Where was Mason calling from? "Shit," he finally said. "I better call her I guess."

"Yeah, that'd be a good idea. Where are you, anyway," I kind of whined. Even on the phone with this stranger I was getting a feeling he didn't respond well to direction or assertive statements. He didn't like being told what to do. Ultimatums.

"I'm....I'm in St. Cloud."

"Yeah? Why is that?"

"Does it matter?"

"It might. If you are in some kind of...Look. Mr. Mason, I'm a private investigator; you know what that is?"

"Well, yeah, I guess."

"I do investigations. Find people. Sometimes provide security for those in some kind of trouble or danger. You understand?" Long pause. Mason thought about what I'd said and I listened to his breathing and the muffled traffic. Finally, another long sigh.

"I understand. Maybe you'd come and get me?"

I said I would, right away, in fact. He named a motel on Highway 10 on the south side of the city. It was about fifty-five miles away, right straight up the highway. Piece of cake.

I threw on some clothes, brushed my teeth and splashed water on my face. At the same time I decided not to wake up my client. I could call her from St. Cloud once I was face to face with Tommy Mason. At the last minute, I packed my tiny airweight .32 revolver into my ankle holster and boogied on out the door. I left lights on in the front hall.

Naturally, except for a few truckers, hauling on up the turnpike, there wasn't much traffic across the northern hump of the Twin Cities. Then I got onto Interstate 94. At Monticello I switched across the river to Highway Ten. Shortly the lights of the strip places along the divided highway near the edge of this sleepy college town disturbed the early morning darkness and soon there it was.

Ten High motel and restaurant, situated right next door to an adult bookstore. I crossed the divide and eased on into the parking area next to the motel office where the lights were on. I killed the engine and looked all around. I didn't see anyone in the lobby, either at the desk, or in the casual chairs. But I couldn't see the whole place. There wasn't anyone lurking in the parking area, either, unless they were hidden in one of the scattering of parked cars nearby.

Mason had declined to provide me with his room number, said he'd wait in the lobby or right outside. I didn't see him. There was nobody and only two cars parked at the long row of white, flat-roofed rooms. I sat there, quietly scanning the surrounding area. I couldn't detect any nearby movement. So I got out of the car. Bent over to retie a shoelace that didn't need it.

I straightened and walked to the side of the building so I could see into the lobby without exposing myself to the light. One divan or sofa was positioned with the back toward me. What I saw was a worn tennis-type shoe, probably a blue and white cross trainer. It was lying upside down on one arm of the sofa. I saw that it was attached to a foot, a sock and part of a pant leg. Then the foot moved and disappeared. I walked to the door and went into the lobby. The door thunked closed behind me and a man with tousled hair sat up and looked toward me with sleep-filled eyes. I recognized him to be Tommy Mason.

"Mr. Mason," I said, extending my right hand. "I'm Sean Sean."

He looked at me, ignored my hand and slowly struggled up off the sofa. His uncertain gaze wandered away and he bent to pick up a tan military-style duffle bag. Then without another word, he started for the door. Apparently he assumed I would follow him. I did. He was the guy I'd come to collect, right?

We went out into the muggy night and I glanced quickly right and left. There were no other creatures abroad at the moment. At least none that I saw. I touched Mason's arm and nodded toward my car. He went to the passenger's side, opened the door and tossed his duffle into the back seat. Then he sat down in the front passenger's seat and closed the door. By that time I'd seated myself behind the wheel and fastened the seat belt.

"The seatbelt works," I said and started the engine. I couldn't see any kind of reaction so I pulled out and drove slowly across the gravel to the highway entrance. It's a split highway so I had to drive a few hundred yards north toward St. Cloud before I could whip a slow U-turn and head back south on the other side. I didn't see any traffic from either direction and no headlights suddenly appeared at the side of the road. We traveled sedately down past the high dour granite walls of the prison, the St. Cloud Minnesota Correctional Institution. Some people called it the Graystone Hotel. Mason turned his head and stared at the walls as we passed.

I gradually increased my speed to the upper limit, keeping a careful eye on the mirrors. If anyone was following us, it was a very loose tail, undetectable that night. Mason didn't say two words the entire hour until I turned south to connect with I-94, which would connect me to I-35, which in turn would take me to the Diamond Lake exit, near where, on South Park, lived Mason's sister.

"What's the deal?" he asked. "Where you takin' me?"

"Your sister's place," I said.

"Why can't I go back to my rooms?"

"You mean to your step-mother's place?"

He glowered at me.

"Work that out with your sister, she's paying for this ride." I'd stopped at a service station in Brooklyn Park and wakened Mason's sister. She'd wanted him delivered to her South Minneapolis home. She'd be waiting, she told me, so that's where we went.

"It's the next one up," he said, when I drew to curb looking for the address Lita'd given me on the telephone.

I glanced over at Tommy. He'd grown less talkative and

seemed surlier as we drove closer to his sister's address. I parked and got out.

As I walked around the car, Tommy seemed to erupt from the passenger seat, screaming. "I can't. I can't go in there." He slammed the door and took off up the sidewalk.

It was still early, for God's sake. Lights came on in dark windows. People would be roused out of bed and somebody would call the cops. That was a complication I didn't need. I legged it up the hill after Tommy. Sweat, in the humid air of the early morning appeared instantly. Shit. Another nice shirt drenched. Well. Maybe I could take it off my taxes.

Tommy wasn't in very good shape, and I do exercise. I have to. My stature dictates that I be ready to run at a moment's notice, especially when I'm not carrying a weapon. I was on him in a quarter of a block.

"Stop, Tommy! Now!" I snapped at him.

He was puffing so hard I'm not sure he heard me. I heard doors slamming down the block behind us and somebody shouted, "Hey." Thanks a lot. One more stride and I tackled him. I grabbed his pants at the back and launched myself at his shoulders, high as I could get. He went down like a pole-axed steer. I think I read that somewhere.

When Tommy fell, he sprawled onto the boulevard grass instead of the sidewalk, thereby avoiding grinding his face into the concrete with my extra one-forty-plus pounds on his back. He gave out a satisfactory grunt as the air left his lungs. I was becoming increasingly irritated with Tommy so I wasn't particularly gentle as I dug a thumb into that very sensitive area of his neck where the nerves run close to the surface. His arm flapped and he gave up all resistance. I snagged a pair of plastic cable ties out of my pocket. I always carry them. They aren't the official police-grade hobbles, but they do just as well on a temporary basis and they cost a heck of a lot less.

I stood up and dragged Tommy to his feet. Hell. I noticed that I'd torn a big hole in my Dockers slacks. More expense. This job was turning into a major irritant. I took Tommy by the elbow and squeezed the joint, just to remind him I knew some other painful pressure points, and started back down the hill toward his sister's front steps. Some helpful citizen puffed up on the slope of his lawn above me and looked down at us. Because I was the better dressed and had the guy in fetters, he addressed himself to me. I guess he assumed I was in charge and I was one of the righteous ones. Ha.

"Need some help, officer?"

"Thanks, but everything's under control," I growled. He nodded and maybe realizing that he was dressed only in a t-shirt, his boxer underwear and flip-flops, he retreated. No other citizens ventured farther than their front stoops. I shoved Tommy to the steps in front of the address I wanted and backed across the lawn to my car where I yanked open the door and retrieved Tommy's duffle bag. I knew Tommy wasn't going to take off again anytime soon.

We went slowly up the steps. Tommy limped a little from his sudden impact with Mother Earth.

His sister stood in the open door and watched us approach.

"Morning, ma'am," I said quietly.

She nodded and stood back a pace, holding the door open for us. We went inside and Tommy slumped onto the couch. I dumped his duffle beside the couch and straightened. I could see right away her main concern and attention was directed at her brother and she was probably a little pissed at my rough handling of Tommy.

"You can use a regular pair of scissors to cut those restraints off his wrists," I said. "He's not drunk and I don't think he's had any drugs for at least twenty-four hours." I stared at the woman. Out of the corner of my eyes I saw Tommy nod his head in apparent agreement. "I'm delivering him per your instructions, but if you want to change your mind, I can charge him with assault for this little dust-up outside your door. They'll keep him for a few hours."

That got a reaction. "Not jail. They'll find me there."

"Who?" I rounded on him and shoved my face close into his. "Who'll find you?" I demanded.

Mason blanched and for the first time since I'd picked him up looked concerned.

"Let me pose a question or two, Mr. Mason." Without waiting, I said, "Looks to me like you're running away from somebody or something, yes? Since I've been on your tail nobody has even come close so it can't be anything major and it isn't the law. Am I right?"

Mason shrugged.

"I'm gonna speculate here and you don't have to say anything." I moved so I was fully in his sight. "I think you are being pressured to do something you don't want to do. Something that's probably illegal. And I bet it's by somebody you are really afraid of. Somebody who you think is protected." I watched Tommy closely. He dropped his eyes and seemed to withdraw. My gut told me I was right on the money.

"Tommy," I said loudly. You stay right here with your sister. I'll take care of Polk." I turned and started for the door. Lita Mason came to me with questions in her eyes.

I shook my head. "Crooked judge, I think. I'll take care of it. Trust me. But don't ask your brother to explain until things are fixed."

She nodded and said, "All right. I'll take care of him now. Thank you."

She took my arm and turned me toward the door. I glanced at her as I went out through the screen. She didn't meet my gaze and she was already closing the door behind me. So that, I figured, was that. Back to my routine. Solving three murders.

29

In spite of being up most of the night and having to deal with a fleeing subject, I felt pretty good after a shower, some clean clothes, and a solid breakfast of homemade buttermilk pancakes slathered with butter, good Canadian maple syrup, plus a couple of thick pieces of crispy bacon on the side. I was rarin' to get back to my rusty revolver. The telephone rang.

"Ann here," she said. "I'm afraid I have some bad news."

"Lay it on me, babe," I growled. She and Catherine were the only two women in my circle I ever called babe. Or ever chanced it. As it was, Catherine occasionally got owl-eyed at me when I uttered it, particularly in the hearing of others.

"DNA analysis. It's pretty messed up, as you'd expect. We found what may be three individuals and one non-human."

"Non-human? Are we dealing with extra-terrestrials here?"

She chuckled softly. "No, dunce. We have a dog, two individuals who appear to be related and you."

"Me."

"Yep. But you understand that none of this is information that will be useable in court. The samples are a real mess, as I said."

"Yeah. Do I assume correctly that the two related individuals are not in your system?"

"You do, but that's probably because these samples are seriously deteriorated. Gotta run. Let me know how it all turns out."

"Sure. Can we not talk out loud about this for a few days?"

"Why, Mr. Sean. Are you asking me to delay this report?"

"Well." I thought fast and decided I wasn't going to trade on my friendship that way. "No, no. I certainly wouldn't suggest anything illegal like that. How long have I got?"

"Two days probably before I get this report to Detective Jackson in White Bear."

"Thanks, Ann. I owe you."

I thought about the revolver and the tests. It had never been a serious threat to my quarry, just a Maguffin that I hoped would cause some turmoil and maybe provoke mistakes. So far so good. Given the travels of the revolver since Spot the dog unearthed it, I assumed Alex's dog had supplied the non-human evidence, that Alex and his father, Kent, were the other two males along with yours truly.

So, off now to run a monumental bluff. I picked up the telephone and called the home of the right dishonorable Judge George Polk. She of the silky smooth southern voice and liquid glide picked up on the third ring.

"Good morning," I offered. "I'd very much like an appointment to see the judge soonest possible. As was the case for the previous two contacts, I'd like to update the judge on the renewed investigation into the great train robbery of 1933."

"Just a moment, sir."

She put the phone down gently. I knew that because I heard no clunk. Of course a lot of these modern digital telephones with their tiny speakers don't carry quite the rich variants of sound that the old heavy black phones out of Bell Labs used to provide. Or maybe my ears are just getting tired.

When she returned, she said, "The judge would be prepared to receive you in one hour, at ten-thirty, if that's convenient."

"Thank you, ma'am. That will be fine."

I went to my basement to my compact but efficient workshop where I retrieved my fine leather holster and my fine small .32

caliber revolver. I unloaded the weapon, checked the trigger and other mechanisms. Then I reloaded the weapon with fresh ammo and strapped it to my ankle.

From my weapons safe I also retrieved my trusty cannon. It's a Colt .45 Caliber semi-automatic handgun. It's heavy and a little awkward for a small man like me to use. It certainly is not something I would use in a quick-draw situation. But I don't get into such shoot-outs, do I? I cleaned and reloaded a magazine. I also took two other loaded magazines which I bundled together in a stout plastic sack. I didn't seriously expect the judge to be waiting on the ramparts in South St. Paul ready for armed conflict. But he had his contacts and I was pretty sure he knew about the recent developments in the case. And he might very well have decided to tell a certain killer where I would be about twenty minutes from now. So I girded, armed, and sallied forth.

As I drove sedately up the final hill to the judge's street, I kept my eyes peeled. I'm not sure what that means, "eyes peeled," but I did it. I ceaselessly check out my surroundings. No untoward movement. No roving bands of gunsels. No roadblocks. No Harlan Ford.

Liquid silk opened the door and silently lead me across the hall and up the curving stairs. This time the judge didn't bother to get to his feet. I glanced cautiously around the room. Judge Polk watched me.

No place for someone to hide in his office. Only the one door. I dragged a chair to the side of his desk so I could see the judge and the door. I wasn't going to sit with my back to the door as I had the last time I visited this office.

"Well, Mr. Sean. Why are you bothering me again?"

"I think you know why, Judge, but as a courtesy, I'll lay it all out for you."

He just looked at me. Today his eyes seemed baleful and reptilian. Funny, I hadn't noticed that before.

"In 1933 your father, the first Judge Polk, was a lawyer on the fast track. It wasn't long before he was made a municipal judge and supervising some important trials here in the city." I smiled, sort of.

"Some of his trials involved the more notorious criminal element that had been attracted to the O'Connor plan which was to make St. Paul a haven for thugs and gangsters as long as they behaved themselves. But when the first Judge Polk was on the bench, some of those gangsters got off lightly, didn't they?"

Polk stirred and looked like he was going to protest, but I bored relentlessly on. "I have a good friend in County Law Enforcement. An attorney. He looked up some old cases. What he found led him to look up your courtroom record as well. He didn't like what he found. You know what he found, don't you. It wasn't a question.

"A pattern is what he found. Interestingly, you'll be glad to learn his last name is also Ford. He's not related to your hired gunny. But we'll get to that. I'm still presenting a short history lesson here." My hip holster was letting the butt of my large gat dig into my side so I shifted in my chair. Rearranged things. Polk didn't say anything, just watched me. I thought he was still breathing.

"Your dad had a secret, didn't he? Comes down to the revolver, doesn't it? I figure he was standing in the window of his law office there on the street when the robbery went down and he saw someone he knew, a relative, no less, shoot that cop, Eddie Washington. But he didn't come forward, did he. He let it slide and then when he got to be a judge, certain people began to talk. Whispers. So he did a few things, made a few rulings one way or another, right? Took a little graft. Right? Along the way he used his influence to corrupt the system, didn't he? And guess what, Judge Polk? Yeah. You found out, or maybe he taught you how, and like daddy like son, the money was good and got even better. What the Hell, right judge? Not too many people got hurt, right?

"But then, last week that damned revolver turned up. It turned up in a hole with a bunch of ruined money. And you could see the whole house of cards falling down around you. Oh, I know, you're off the bench and you just want to be left alone to live here in this place built by two corrupt judges, you and your daddy. Right? Quietly for the rest of your days."

So far the judge hadn't said anything, but he was paying attention. I was conscious that my voice was rising. I was irritated and I was excited. This jerk had had three people killed. "So you reached back into your files and you found a thug who could be bought. You found Harlan Ford."

Polk blinked. I knew I'd guessed right. I pressed on.

"You hired Ford to find out what was happening in the Kavas' back yard and then when your niece...." I stopped, took a deep breath and then went on at a lower volume. "Your niece, Kristi Polk Kava, for God's sake, figured out what it was about after the revolver was dug up. She came to see you, didn't she? She told you about the weapon and the money. So you directed Ford to lay me out and find out what else might be in the hole."

I was angry at this old fool because I was sure he'd had his own relatives murdered to protect his name and reputation. I was also upset because I realized that if Ford had laid hands on the buried money and the rusty iron, the judge would have discovered that it was all untraceable and that would have ended it. Two civilians and the dead cop would probably still be alive.

But Alex's mom had told the old man that she thought the gun could be traced and that really tore it. I stood up suddenly and slammed my chair back. The old judge seemed to shrivel as I leaned over his desk. I planted both sweaty hands on his shiny desk top and snarled, "I'm gonna find Harlan Ford now and if I have to break his thumbs, I'll get a confession out of him. You're going to jail for your sins, you rat."

I admit I can't deliver a line like that with the gravitas of a

Sydney Greenstreet, say, or Richard Widmark, but I made my point. I could see it in his face. I pivoted on my heel and walked across his carpet to the door. I went out without looking back, closing the door softly behind me. The house was very quiet, very cool, very dark.

30

It was hot that day. I remember that it was one of the hottest days of the summer, and even with the air cranked as high as it would go, the metal surfaces of the Taurus were uncomfortable to the touch. I motored down the bluff through South St. Paul. I'd reached the bottom of the bluff when a local squad, lights flashing, siren screaming through the hot air, passed me, heading up the hill in the opposite direction I was coming from.

I drove to my office in Minneapolis. There were no messages to deal with. The mail had been delivered and I dealt with that in about twenty minutes. Then I picked up the phone and called the PD in South St. Paul. When I gave the operator my name, he connected me directly with Chief Johnson's office. His assistant put me through right away.

"Chief Johnson," I said. I didn't identify myself; I figure the assistant had already done that. "I'm ninety percent sure Judge Polk is behind the murders of the Kavas in White Bear Lake and of your detective, Tom McKinley. What I know probably isn't enough for a prosecution to go forward but that'll come when I lay hands on Harlan Ford."

"He's dead." the chief interrupted. "Judge Polk committed suicide this afternoon. Just about an hour ago, it looks like. You know anything about it?"

"Yeah, I do," I said and told him about my conversation with the corrupt dead judge.

"Uh huh," he said in my ear. "He left some files out on the desk and a long typed note or letter. It pretty much confirms what you just told me. We've issued an arrest warrant for Ford."

"I'll be talkin' to you soon, Chief." I cradled the instrument, cutting off whatever he'd started saying. I wanted Harlan Ford in the worst way. For my own perverse reasons I wanted him before official law swallowed him up. I called Catherine and left a message that I didn't know when I'd see her next. I figured that as soon as the news got around, Ford would be in the wind. I figured I had maybe two hours to lay hands on him before he split for good or the cops found him.

* * * *

I drove my hot tired car across the baking urban landscape to Ford's last known address. When I banged on the door, I could see that the bell had still not been repaired. I stepped to one side and gave the heavy door my best cop rap. The one that seems to demand instant response, or maybe flight.

I heard heavy steps and a muttering as the door was flung open to crash against the wall. I stepped in front of Harrison and pointed my big .45 at his face. He flinched and turned both hands outward so I could see his grimy empty palms. I was standing in the classic gunfighter pose, arms outstretched at shoulder height, elbows locked, both hands cradling the weapon like it was a newborn babe.

"Ford," I said quietly. Is he here? If not where? How long has he been gone? Don't give me any shit. Just none at all. I'm on a very short fuse here."

"Easy, man, easy." Harrison flinched again and tried to step to one side, away from the big hole of the barrel of my weapon. I tracked him, the weapon aimed perfectly at the center of his nose. He started to sweat. Beads of moisture tracked down the sides of his face.

"He ain't here, he left maybe an hour ago and he prob'ly went up north."

"If you're screwin' with me, I won't kill you, I'll just find you and put one through your knee."

"Jesus, man," he whined. "Lighten up. It's the God's truth. I ain't involved with him. We don't hang together. His sister lives in Sunrise, or a little east of there, anyway."

I was ninety percent certain Harrison was being truthful. I slid the weapon back into my hip holster and whirled around. As I jumped off the porch, he called after me, "He's got a gun. He took my Winchester."

I stopped and looked back at him. "Scoped rifle?"

"Yeah."

"That's probably the weapon that killed Detective McKinley."

"No shit!" Apparently news to Harrison.

I ran for my car.

I had no hope of catching Ford before he reached Sunrise and I didn't know his route. I drove to Roseville and grabbed a rifle and some loaded magazines for it, plus a spray can of Deep Woods Off and spare ammo for my .45. I threw it all in my car along with a couple bottles of water. I left a quick call at the apartment so Catherine wouldn't worry. In minutes, with the sun hanging low over my left side, I was haulin' ass up I-35W toward Forest Lake.

Sunrise was fifty plus miles north and east of me. The little town took its name from the Sunrise River, a creek, really, that feeds into the St. Croix River. That's the river that forms a boundary between most of Minnesota and Wisconsin. Somebody designated it a wild river, meaning most human depredations are limited and people canoe and camp and fish on it. I knew the territory only slightly but I could follow a map. One of my detective skills.

I went up the interstate, to North Branch (no idea where Branch might be) where I hung a sharp right on State Highway 95.

I thought about contacting the Chisago County sheriff, but what would I tell him? That I was chasing an armed felon on the run from at least three murders in the Twin Cities, but I couldn't prove my allegations? Didn't see much point.

A little way east of town is a paved County Highway, number 9. It runs right into Sunrise, a small community of around 1,600 folks. I drove sedately through town, eyes peeled for Ford's Chevy. I didn't have the license number, but McMillan has told me it was an older white four-door sedan with a rear passenger side door that was yellow. Apparently Ford had replaced a back door with one from another vehicle. I didn't see the car on my first pass. I did see a lot of big pine trees, the meandering creek, a scattering of homes, and a cemetery.

Half a mile north of the town limit, according to a well-shot-up sign, was a roadhouse. You know the kind. You find 'em in lots of detective novels. They're dark and smoky and in the middle of the afternoon several evil-looking characters are in there, lounging at the bar. These are characters with no discernable means of support and when you walk in they stare at you as if they'd like to tear you apart.

Wrong. This place was called Sunrise. It had lots of windows, it smelled fresh and clean and the woman behind the bar looked like your average Scandinavian. She was big, buxom and had a lot of bright white teeth that she flashed at me in a big grin. There wasn't anyone else in the place.

I sat down and ordered a glass of beer. Budweiser was on tap, she said.

"I'm a stranger here," I said, taking a long swallow. The temperature of the beer was just right, a few degrees above ice.

"I can see that," she replied. "We're pretty well off the highway here so we mostly get local folks. And, if you don't mind my saying so, you're the first grown man I've seen in a long time wearing red tennis shoes."

"No, I don't mind. I'm up here from Minneapolis on business. Maybe you can tell me how to find Miriam Ford's place." Sometimes the direct approach is the best one.

"Ah," she said. "I suppose it's her brother again."

"You know Harlan?"

"Yep. Most everybody knows that troublemaker. You a cop?"

"Not exactly. My information is that Harlan came up here today, to his sister's place."

"He sure did," she said. "That's his pattern. He gets into trouble and runs home to his older sister for help. He was in here not more'n an hour ago. Bought a bottle of whiskey and some chips. He'll be gettin' drunk, I imagine, at the house. It's the weatherbeaten blue rambler. You go south to the cemetery and turn left. Fourth house down the road on the right. Can't miss it. Miriam works in St. Paul so she won't be home for 'nother hour at least."

"Thanks," I said and drained my glass. "Well-kept draft," I remarked and exited.

She was right. When I turned left at the cemetery I could see Ford's beat-up Chevy with the one yellow door parked in the yard of a blue rambler just down the street. So I pulled my .45 out of its holster and laid it in my lap. Then I idled slowly along the unpaved road. My plan was to wait patiently for about another hour in the hopes that Ford would drink away the afternoon and I could handcuff him with a minimum of hassle, just before his sister arrived home. But things didn't work out that way.

I cruised slowly by, scanning the rambler without staring at the place. Just as I got opposite the small front porch, the figure of a man appeared at the front door. He hesitated a moment. It looked as though he was staring right at me, but I couldn't be sure. He disappeared inside as I rolled a little farther. When I looked back over my left shoulder, Harlan Ford was bolting out of the front door into the yard. The screen door crashed back as he took a flying leap off the steps, staggered, and then flung himself into the car.

I floored the accelerator and made a cloud-raising skidding about face, front tires spinning madly. By the time I got straightened out and back to the house, Ford was a quarter-block ahead, roaring madly up the road spitting his own plume of dust. He fishtailed onto the highway and sped south out of Sunrise.

31

His vehicle had a better engine and he steadily gained on me, but he was still in sight when he careened east on 95, almost losing control as he made the turn. I did a beautiful four-wheel drift through the corner, plowing almost blind through the cloud of dust he'd raised, and gained appreciatively. We shot through light traffic, weaving as we went. He didn't gain much over the next couple of miles. His car had softer springing and I'm a better driver. In spite of his superior engine power, I was able to hang with him.

At Almelund, he grabbed a sudden left, narrowly missing a metallic blue Neon coming west. Fortunately none of the citizens of the little community were on the streets and Ford blew up County Highway 12 for about half a mile, past the grocery store and the big church. He was out of sight for a moment, but when I got to the intersection with Highway 16, I saw fresh tracks of a vehicle that had skidded across the intersection and into the deep ditch. There were also tracks coming out of the ditch. I glanced down the road, thankful there were no other cars or farm vehicles close by coming the other way. As I turned east on 16, I thought briefly about high speed chases and how they too often ended in tragedy. Then I wiped the sweat off with one hand and pressed harder on the accelerator which was already flat against the firewall. The engine whined and I heard a funny sound, like some piece of metal was over-stressed and about to give out. I flew over a small rise in the road, the fields on either side long smears of mottled green.

I didn't look at the speedometer. I didn't want to scare myself. The car floated over another hill and seemed to lose its grip on the road. My stomach floated too. I roared after the fleeing Chevy, down a hill and up. Across an empty intersection. Half a mile ahead, glinting through the trees, the road seemed to disappear. I saw a flash of blue and realized we were roaring right toward the river. There's no bridge at that location. No old railroad or ancient buggy bridge. He'd have to go south nine winding miles along the river to get to a bridge.

The white Chevy suddenly seemed to juke left then right, then left again, raising clouds of dirt as it fishtailed on the gravel shoulders. It disappeared. A tractor nosed into the road from the right, then stopped. Ford must have flinched. I screamed up, pounding on the brake pedal and saw the guy on the tractor standing and pointing left across the road, his mouth hanging open. There were skid marks on the pavement heading toward a ragged gap in the underbrush.

I stood on the brakes and slewed the Taurus to a smoking stop at the side of the road, just at the lip of a long downward line of pavement through the encroaching trees. A roughly paved, narrow track led at right angles into the brush. It bridged a deep ravine with a kind of saddle that separated the road from the land to the north. When I got out of the car, I saw the back end of the white Chevy, on its side among crushed bushes and small trees at the bottom of the ravine. Except for the ticking of cooling metal, it was quiet.

The farmer had shut off his tractor and come over to where I was standing staring at my target. "Jezus! That guy almost took out my tractor. He tried to make it up that driveway. I guess I musta startled him."

"I guess so," I said.

"You a cop?"

"Something like that. You didn't see him after he went over the edge?"

"Nope."

"He's armed, so don't go over there. You got a cell phone?"

"Sure."

"Call 911," I said. I reached into the front seat of my car and hauled out my gat. It had fallen on the floor during the chase. Motioning the farmer to go back to his tractor, I ducked and scuttled across the highway toward the back of the Chevy. Sweat trickled down my face and I started to smell my fear. I hated these situations plus I didn't have a whole lot of experience with them. Mickey Spillane I am not.

When I slid down the slope to the back of the Chevy, pistol pointed ahead, I stopped and listened. Only heard heat-related sounds. Critters in the vicinity were still in shocked silence. There wasn't any breeze and I heard no groans, no cries, no sobs and no heavy breathing except my own. I risked a peek around the back fender at the front driver's side door. It was shut and from the look if would require a wrecker and the Jaws of Life to get it open. I scrabbled to the other side of the car, hard to do on a steep bank when one hand is clutching a heavy semi-automatic.

The passenger-side door was open, wide open. In fact it was wrapped partway around a young tree that stuck up near the front fender on that side. "Ford," I said. "Are you in there?"

No answer. I figured he was either unconscious or dead. Turned out he was neither. What Ford was, was gone. There wasn't much blood. And no rifle. There was a box of 30-06 metal-jacketed shells spilled on the front floorboards. The windshield was intact and badly cracked, so he hadn't been ejected. He'd been incredible lucky. I searched around the front of the car and found what looked like a fresh set of scars on the steep hillside leading up to the land. They looked exactly like the kind of scars somebody would make climbing desperately up that hill, grabbing bushes and clawing for progress. Now the mosquitoes had found me. I scrambled back up to the pavement.

"What's up there?" I asked the farmer who was leaning against the front of his green John Deere tractor.

"Nothin' much. It used to be crop fields and pasture. John Bjork used to farm it. Ran a few cows on it years ago. The guy who owns it lives in the Cities."

"No house or cabin?"

"Nope. The city folks built some kind of weird round place up in the middle, maybe a quarter mile."

"You mean like a geodesic dome?"

"Yep. They never had any electricity or water and the building went down a few years ago. Tree fell on it. They planted trees in the fields after Johnny quit farming."

"Trees," I said.

"Yeah, oaks and white pines." He pointed up the overgrown driveway. Lotta deer there too. And maybe a bear."

"Really," I said.

"See, the land butts up against Wild River State Park. The park runs down the bluff to the river right over there." He pointed again.

"How far is the park headquarters, would you say?"

"Three-four miles, maybe."

"Okay," I said. "Thanks. Can you wait here for the sheriff? Tell them I'm in there looking for a guy named Harlan Ford."

"He any kin to Miriam, up to Sunrise?"

I stared at the farmer. "Her brother. You know him?"

He shook his head. "Nope, but his sister goes to our church in Almelund."

"Thanks for your help," I said and shook his hard calloused hand. Then I went to the trunk of my car and took out the can of bug spray, a blue Twins baseball cap, and another magazine for the .45. I stuffed my small binoculars in a back pocket. I debated myself about whether to carry my rifle.

I was going after a guy who knew the woods better than I did and he had a scoped rifle, if Harrison was to be believed. But he was desperate, might be injured and wouldn't hesitate to kill again, I figured. I wanted to get him so no more innocent people would be hurt. True, it was personal as well. I was sure the bullet that took out detective McKinley in South St. Paul was meant for me. I put my arm through the sling and shouldered the long gun.

I lifted one hand to the farmer and walked through the saddle and up the overgrown driveway. When I got to the top of the incline, I almost turned back. The ragged rows of tall white pines were close together and seemed to stretch forever up the field toward who knew what. A fence at the park boundary, I supposed. On my right there was a gap of about ten feet between the trees and the bushes at the edge of the property. I went to a position above the place where the Chevy now rested and sure enough, there were faint tracks of crushed weeds and broken branches. It was Ford's trail right into the heart of the grove of trees.

It stood to reason, I thought, that he knew something about the area and would try to find new transportation somewhere in the park. That meant a trek of several miles through the woods and fields. But if he was hurt from running his car into the ditch, I might catch him before he got too far. Alas, my woodsman's tracker skills were non-existent but I figured I might get lucky. Or I might just get shot.

I gave myself a liberal spraying of bug repellant, holstered my handgun and trudged into the forest. These woods were old enough to have lost a few limbs and shed lots of needles, but not mature enough so that the undergrowth was stunted. Give me an urban slum anytime. It was tough going through thick weeds and over hidden limbs and it was hotter than Hell in there. I figured I had about three or four hours of decent daylight left. If I waited too long to come out of the woods, either the local authorities would have to find me, or I'd just hunker down and wait for daylight. Neither was a pleasant prospect.

I stumbled through the forest, cursing Ford, myself, the gods in general, all the while steaming sweat. I thought I had been out there for hours, but when I reached the crest of a small hill, still surrounded by pine woods, I stopped to rest and looked at my watch. Only forty-five minutes had passed. Going down the gentle slope was easier and the trees were a little thinner. Ahead I could see where the forest petered out and the tall grass began in earnest. I never heard the shot that took a piece off my left ear.

32

The hard smack on the side of my head knocked my hat off and sent me flat to the ground. Then a stinging sensation made itself known and grew into a sizeable headache. When I hit the ground, cushioned by the thick weedy grass, I'd instinctively drawn my weapon. I pointed the .45 ahead of me and peered over the sight though sweat-filled eyes. There was nothing out of place to be seen. After a moment, I put my hand to my ear. That hurt more and my fingers came away bloody. I was scared for a moment but then I realized that I wasn't dead and I could still hear out of both ears. I touched my left ear again and found more blood. Not a lot of blood. The rifle was digging into my side.

I cursed and rolled to my left and found a tree with a thick enough trunk that was screened from the next grove of trees and underbrush about seventy yards north across a scrubby path of tall weeds. I was in the tall weeds, that's for sure. I stood slowly holding myself sideways behind the comforting bulk of the tree. Because I'm short, my head cleared the tall grass in the open field in front of me by only a few inches.

The sun was behind me and as it got lower it would be in Ford's eyes, if he was looking and not running. I looked over the grove across the field. I saw something that didn't look natural, but I couldn't be sure what it was. I jammed my Winchester against the tree trunk and cut loose. A single shot. The weapon bucked and I dropped to the ground. There was no answering fire. Now what?

I could work my way north to the bluff through this hand-planted forest. Tough hot going, until I reached the older oak grove on the bluff itself. Then I could cut around to the east and maybe flank him. If I could do that maybe Ford would have to retreat toward the road. That would drive him into the arms of the sheriff. That was if he stayed where he was. Where he was, I thought, might be in the ruins of that collapsed dome the owners had built.

I stood up again behind my tree. The sun sank lower in the sky as the world turned. I considered my options again. There weren't many and none of them were attractive. I scuttled farther north, up the gentle slope, skipping from tree to tree. There was just enough dead grass and fallen needles and small limbs to make walking difficult. I stopped and put the glasses on the place where I thought Ford might be holed up.

Now I could see down a sort of path the owner must have cut to the site of the dome from the edge of the field. Part of the ru-ined structure was visible. Behind me faintly at first then increasingly louder I heard the sound of sirens. Many sirens. The cavalry was approaching. I knew Ford could hear them too. Unless he had gone on down the bluff toward the river and the park. Maybe he didn't know about the park.

The siren sounds peaked and then died away. A little while later I heard voices coming closer. One voice called my name several times. Since the voices came from the direction of the road, I assumed they were friendlies. "Hello," I called. "I'm over here."

"Sean Sean?" a young sounding voice responded.

"That's me. Come north a bit. Up the slope."

"Hang on." The youthful sounding voice soon matched up with a young and slender blonde in a Chisago County deputy sheriff uniform. The deputy, sweat running down his cheeks, sank down beside me and said, "What's the situation? We've had some conversation with the PD in White Bear Lake about you and this fellow you're chasing. Harlan Ford? Killed some folks down there? I'm Karl, by the way, with a K." He stuck out a big soft hand and we shook.

"Right. Listen. I have some history with this guy. Maybe I can talk him out. Have you got a bull horn or loud speaker?

"Sure. Hang on." Karl with a K pressed a button on a black mike stuck on his shoulder and requested somebody bring up a loud hailer. Then he pulled out a county map and we figured out where we were and how to secure the area.

"The guy is probably injured from when he wrecked his car. If he knows he can't get away maybe he'll come out peaceably," I said.

"Any shots fired?" the deputy asked.

"Two. He fired at me and almost took my head off." I showed him my blood-clotted ear, "and I fired back, basically a blind shot." I looked at his map again. "What's over here?" I traced my finger over a wide swath of country across the river in Wisconsin.

"Open country. Highway here. Not a populated area. Coupla farms. South side here is the ski park. Up here is the area where there'll be some campers in Wild River State Park. We sent a car there already. And there's patrols along the road out here down to the river."

I nodded. "So he's cut off from everything but the river."

Another deputy arrived carrying a battery powered megaphone-like loud hailer and a rifle. As he squatted beside us, another shot cracked overhead through the trees. It showered a few pine needles down on us. They smelled sweet for a few moments. Instinctively we all ducked our heads. I reached for the loud hailer and switched it on. It crackled loudly.

Staying on the ground, I pointed the cone uphill and called, "Ford. Harlan Ford." It sounded just like it does in the movies. "Ford, this is Sean Sean, the detective you met outside your apartment?" Actually, I'd put a gun on him that time, but I figured I didn't want to remind him of how we first met in the Kavas' back yard. "You're surrounded, man. Let's give it up and nobody gets hurt. Night's coming and the mosquitoes are gonna get really bad out here. We'll be scratching for weeks."

I glanced around and caught the deputies smirking at each other. So it was a little unorthodox. Whatever worked, I figured. It didn't seem to. For a few seconds there was silence and then several shots whined overhead and slammed into trees around us.

"I'm supposed to go back to the command ... the driveway. Mr. Sean, I'm supposed to bring you along," said the second deputy, the one who'd brought the loudhailer.

"Forget it," I said. "This guy killed my client and left a kid orphaned. He murdered a deputy while aiming at me. He's got a debt to pay and I'm the collector."

The deputy nodded and scuttled away down the hill into the thick trees saying, "I'll pass the message along."

I hunkered down again and looked at my companion, the other deputy. Karl-with-a-K shrugged and said, "Kind of a stalemate. But eventually we'll probably get someone in a position to take him out. How'd we get here, anyway?"

"A long time ago, back in 1933, there was a train robbery in South St. Paul," I began. I unshipped my binocs and made myself comfortable against the tree. I could just see the ruined dome over the grass in the clearing ahead, so Ford couldn't move without notice, unless he was already headed down the slope northeast toward the river.

"The robbers killed a rookie cop on their way out of town. One of the thieves, probably the one who shot the cop, was related to a lawyer in town. He may have seen the shooting, or not, but in any case he never said anything. He became a judge and later his son became a judge. It looks to me and to the South St. Paul police as if that secret about the cop killing altered the judge's views of life and justice. And when a relative found a rusty pistol along with some loot from the robbery, the judge thought the whole house of cards was gonna collapse. So he hired our friend Harlan Ford up there to take out the people who found the weapon, because the woman, Kristi Kava, must have figured out where the revolver came from. And because I began to make a public stink about it.

"So you've been chasing this guy, Harlan Ford?"

"Yeah, as soon as I made a connection between Ford and Judge Polk, I was sure I had my guy."

I went on to explain the twisting path I'd followed to get to this miserable hot patch of weeds, whacking at the growing cloud of mosquitoes between sentences. I wished I still smoked. It might have driven the critters away. The shadows were getting longer. I continued my story.

"Anyway, I—hey! He's running!" I lurched to my feet and raised my weapon, resting it against the tree. Ford was running down the hill bent over to make a smaller target. I fired. Missed but Ford hesitated so I aimed a little lower.

Behind me Deputy Karl screamed into the loud hailer, "South! Toward the road! He's runnin' south!"

I fired and for a moment I thought I'd lost him. Then I could see Ford through the weeds, springing up again. He'd lost the rifle and I bolted out of the trees after him at a dead run. The deputy screamed again into the bullhorn but I couldn't make out the words. Then I heard him pounding after me. Sweat poured off my head and ran into my eyes. I'm in pretty good shape but this was ridiculous. Running over the bumpy field, I caught my foot on a gopher mound or something and went head over ass. When I bounded up, Harlan Ford was trying to get up again and stumble away. He groaned and went down on his face. I could see fresh blood on his pants. My second shot had nicked him in the calf. A nick from a rifle slug is no small matter. The bullet had taken his leg right out from under him. I didn't know where his rifle was or whether Ford had a pistol somewhere on him. I jumped forward and fell on his back. Later they told me I was screaming.

Ford whooshed and groaned when I landed between his shoulder blades.

"Just stay there," I puffed. I dragged my Colt up and ground it into his side. Ford went limp.Deputy Karl stumbled up and efficiently wrapped Ford's wrists with steel. I rolled off the guy and looked up at the darkening sky. Through our heavy breathing, I heard the grinding sound of a jeep laboring across the field toward us. The Cavalry had arrived.

33

"May I provide you with another drink, my liege?" Catherine snaked a slender arm across my shoulder, reached for my tumbler. Interesting word that, to describe a short heavy glass made for holding spirits. Anyway, Catherine was murmuring in my ear, my un-injured ear, with that very subtle edge to her voice.

Most of the time she approves of my professional activities, because she recognizes that I'm usually helping people. Chasing armed felons over weedy fields is not an approved tactic. I came home two nights ago with a lot of scratches from the underbrush, a few random marks from my scuffle with Mr. Ford, and several muscle aches from unaccustomed activity. I do try to stay in reasonable shape, but tumbling about with said felon stretched a few tendons in unaccustomed ways. So I was complaining under my breath. And Catherine was showing a bare minimum of sympathy.

"I still don't see why you couldn't have just watched him go, instead of rushing out and tackling their guy," she said, handing me another drink of cool amber single malt.

"As I explained, had Ford made it to the gully between the road and the field, he might have slipped away. More likely, one of the cops who were roaring up would have plugged him. Had he been plugged, he could have died and we'd not have his confession."

"But you already told me he didn't know much."

"True, except for two key pieces. He confirmed what I suspected, that he was sent to the Kavas' home the first time to try to retrieve the revolver. He also confirmed he was hired by Judge Polk to get the weapon, and when that didn't happen the first time, Polk sent him back to search the Kava home. It's just too damn tragic that they surprised him during his search.

"Not to change the subject, my dear, but what's the latest word on the nameless caller?"

"Your friends did a good job. It was some religious nut. The electronics guy identified him a couple of days ago."

"Why was I not made privy to this information?"

"You were busy with your case and I thought we could handle it. As it turns out, we did"

"We did?"

Catherine smiled. "We did. Your electronics guy has a friend. A wild man." I opened my mouth to say something, but Catherine interfered by pressing a finger to my lips. "He used to play defense for the Wild. The Minnesota pro Hockey team?"

I nodded. Of course I knew who the Wild were.

"This ex-pro hockey player paid a little visit to my caller to advise him to quit or suffer physical pain."

"Really."

"Yes, really. Now tell me again why the revolver was so important." She grinned and I smiled back.

"In spite of the fact that the weapon was useless as evidence, Polk and Ford didn't know that. Polk and his father, the other Judge Polk, knew that the weapon had been used by his father's nephew to kill the cop, Eddie Washington, during the Railway Express robbery."

"What happened to that guy?"

"That Polk?" I said, taking a sip of scotch. "He disappeared and there are no local records of him ever being arrested. I'm certain, although I can't prove it, that John P buried the revolver and a sack of loot right after the heist. Probably that very night."

"How do you know he shot Eddie Washington?"

"Again, can't prove it in court, but I found a picture in the Historical Society files that show John Polk holding the revolver moments after he shot Washington. Polk's back is to the camera, but I just know it's him."

"Part of the reason you know is because of that strange contact with the attorney, George Van Buren. Am I right?'

"I don't understand how Van Buren happens to have some kind of inside information," Catherine said, sliding down on the couch beside me so her long slender body came into total loving contact with myself.

"I confess, I don't either. Maybe it was something Ford told him. Or maybe, because he also knew Judge Polk, the good judge had used Van Buren's services, or maybe he just let something slip. I understand he and the Judge occasionally played poker together."

"More speculation, huh?"

"Yep. What I know for sure is that justice will be laid on a killer, a kid will grow up without his parents but in the care of a loving aunt, and a corrupt judge ended his days in personal if not public disgrace."

"A useless piece of iron, a Maguffin, caused a lot of harm," Catherine murmured.

"Unintended consequences of thoughtless action," I murmured back, rolling toward her so I could nuzzle her smooth warm neck.

"No such here, not tonight," she murmured.

OTHER WORKS BY CARL BROOKINS

Short Stories

"Night Sail," *The Pinehurst Journal*, 1992.
"A Winter's Tale," *Silence of The Loons*, 2005.
"Hard Cheese," e-book, 2005.
"A Winter's Tale," e-book, 2005.
"A Fish Story," *Resort to Murder*, 2007.
"Daddy's Little Girl," 2011.
"The Day I Lost My Innocence," 2011.
"The Horse He Rode In On," *Fifteen Tales of Murder, Mayhem, and Malice: from the Land of Minnesota Nice*, 2012.

Novels

THE SAILING MYSTERY SERIES

Inner Passages, Top Publications, 2000.
A Superior Mystery, Top Publications, 2002.
Old Silver, Top Publications, 2005.
Devils Island, Echelon Publications, 2010.
Red Sky, e-Book, Brookins Books, 2011.

THE DETECTIVE SERIES

The Case of the Yellow Diamond, North Star Press of Saint Cloud, Mn, 2015.
The Case of the Deceiving Don, Five Star Mysteries Press, 2008.
The Case of the Greedy Lawyers, Nodin Press, 2008.
The Case of the Great Train Robbery, Brookins Books, 2011.
The Case of the Missing Case, e-Book, Brookins Books, 2012.
The Case of the Purloined Painting, North Star Press of Saint Cloud, 2013.

THE ACADEMIC SERIES

Bloody Halls, Echelon Press, 2008.
Reunion, Echelon Press, 2011.

www.ingramcontent.com/pod-product-compliance
Lightning Source LLC
Chambersburg PA
CBHW060926180626
46817CB00004B/1416